Remarkab
the Bess Cr

"[Readers] are bound to be caught up in the adventures of Bess Crawford . . . The strong-willed and self-determined daughter of a retired colonel, Bess shows her mettle . . . While her sensibility is as crisp as her narrative voice, Bess is a compassionate nurse who responds with feeling."

—*The New York Times Book Review*

"Intensely personal, as all great stories should be."

—Anne Perry,
Internationally Bestselling Author

"Sensitive, beautifully written, disconcertingly familiar."

—*Kirkus Reviews*

"Another Charles Todd book is always a luscious treat."

—Historical Novel Society

"Charles Todd has developed believable characters that carry along this story with lightning speed from the first page to the last."

—*New York Journal of Books*

"Bess is among the most compassionate and intelligent characters, whose observations on life and people are advanced for the era in which she lives."

—*The Sun-Sentinel* (Florida)

"The Todds excel at complex characterizations . . . A sweet treat indeed." —*Wilmington Star-News* (North Carolina)

"As always, the mother-son writing team of Charles Todd does a magnificent job with atmosphere and dialogue, all while keeping their good-hearted heroine one step (but only one) ahead of the bad guys." —BookPage

"A gripping whodunit haunted by the brutal realities of war and graced with the selfless determination of Bess to uncover the truth." —*Richmond Times-Dispatch*

"As usual, Todd mixes historical verisimilitude with exemplary character design and sharp plotting." —*Booklist*

"Fans of historical mysteries who have not yet read the Bess Crawford series by the writing duo known as Charles Todd should do so immediately." —All About Romance

"Terrific . . . There are still plenty of stories left for Bess Crawford, and I cannot wait to see what happens next."

—BookReporter.com

A Hanging at Dawn

Also by Charles Todd

A Hanging at Dawn

A Bess Crawford Short Story

CHARLES TODD

WITNESS
IMPULSE

An Imprint of HarperCollinsPublishers

Excerpt from *A Fatal Lie* copyright © 2021 by Charles Todd.

Digital Edition NOVEMBER 2020 ISBN: 978-0-06-304856-0
Print Edition ISBN: 978-0-06-304857-7

Cover design by Guido Caroti
Cover photographs © Pikoso.kz/Shutterstock (temple); © Mia Stendal/Shutterstock (fog); © Laura Crazy/Shutterstock (fog)

FIRST EDITION

21 22 23 24   LSC   10 9 8 7 6 5 4 3

Author's Note

WHEN WE WERE well along in our Ian Rutledge series, we wrote a short story "prequel" to explore Hamish MacLeod's life before the books began: *The Piper*.

We did the same thing for the Bess Crawford series, with a short story about Bess growing up in India, well before the books caught up with her: *The Maharani's Pearls*.

And now here, in *A Hanging at Dawn*, is a short story about Simon Brandon, who figures large in the Bess Crawford series—filling in some of the blanks that the reader doesn't know. Secrets even Bess herself doesn't know. Yet.

But you needn't be a fan of either series to read these prequels. They are complete in themselves and—we hope!—each a great story on its own.

Enjoy!

A Hanging at Dawn

Prologue

England, the turn of the century...

Who is this man, Simon Brandon, and why has his past been a
blank to those who think they know him best?

Was it something in Simon himself—or something in the people
around him, seeing what they wanted to see—that made him the
man he was?

Why did Melinda Crawford, widow of a British Army officer, step
in at a crucial moment in Simon's life, and then for his pride's sake,
step away? Why did she give her cousin, Richard Crawford, recently
promoted Major in a regiment posted to India, the daunting task of
turning the angry boy—if possible—into a man and a soldier?

What was there about him that made Clarissa, Richard's wife,
trust him with their small daughter, Bess?

Was it his own youth or something else in him that made Bess tease
and bully him to get her own way—and unwittingly teach him to laugh?

What was there about him that made a handful of people stand
by him until the end, when he was in dire straits and facing death?

Melinda

I HAD JUST returned from a spring visit to Florence. As the staff greeted me, my attention was suddenly caught by the post lying in the silver dish, where it is always left during my absence. There was a crest on the topmost letter that I immediately recognized, and after responding to my welcome, I walked over to pick it up.

It was from a dear friend, a high-ranking member of the General Staff, Harris Clifford.

And it had been posted a week ago.

Curious, I picked it up and opened it at once, drawing out the single sheet inside.

And it was a very good thing I did! Because Harris had written to inform me that he would be arriving—*Great heavens—* *today at* *two o'clock.*

I glanced up at the tall case clock face. *That was ten minutes from now.*

There was no time for a bath, no time even to bring in the rest of my trunks. I had hardly taken off my hat, brushed the travel wrinkles out of my skirts, before a *pair* of horses came trotting up my drive.

If my late husband hadn't stood unequivocally against women using strong language, I would have sworn. I certainly knew how, and I was fairly certain my vocabulary was the equal of any trooper in the line. Nevertheless, I did try to honor his memory.

I sent the staff away, handed my hat and gloves and traveling cloak to Shanta, who whisked them out of sight, and then hastily climbed the stairs.

From the window overlooking the drive, I watched as the Colonel and a junior officer dismounted and came striding up to knock at my door.

Not a social call, then, or the Colonel would have come alone.

I must say, Harris Clifford had not changed with the years. Tall, broad-shouldered, handsome—and a fine soldier. He'd been decorated for bravery more than once. His hair was streaked with gray now, but in my view it only added to his charm.

I turned away and stepped quietly into my sitting room.

Shanta came upstairs, knocked lightly at my door, and announced my visitors.

"They are in the parlor, two very handsome officers. Why did you not come home sooner? Look at you! Let me straighten your skirts!"

She has been with me for more years than I cared to count, and she still addresses me as if I am ten.

"It won't do any good—I shall just have to make the best of it."

Resigned, I went down the stairs and into the drawing room, where Harris and the junior officer were waiting.

"My dear," he said, coming forward to take my hands and kiss me on both cheeks. "It's wonderful to see you. You're looking well—as always!"

I smiled up at him. "And I see that the Army still agrees with you."

He grimaced. "Occasionally." Keeping one of my hands in his, he turned. "May I present Major MacInnes. Of your old Regiment."

The Major was perhaps thirty-five, an attractive man, and, as I discovered, with a lovely Scottish accent.

He bowed formally, saying, "It's a pleasure to meet you, ma'am. We still talk about your services in India."

I hadn't intended to be a heroine. But at the Siege of Lucknow, we'd been evacuated from the city itself to the Residency, and we were hard-pressed to hold out until help arrived. I'd taken water out to the men holding the perimeter against the mutineers, and because I was small, I'd managed to reach a good many of them without being shot at. Of course, it hadn't actually occurred to me that I might be shot at, I was just six. My only thought was to relieve the thirst of men who were literally protecting us from a fate worse than death at the hands of rebels who took evil pleasure in the savage mutilation of women and children. But my poor mother, watching me move along the line, had her heart in her throat. The heat in India takes a terrible toll of body and then soul, and I had worried about those soldiers. Most of whom I knew, because my own father was somewhere else in India, fighting to quell the Mutiny and relieve places like Lucknow. The history books called it the Sepoy Rebellion, spreading across India like wildfire when Muslim troops were told that their rifle cartridges had deliberately been smeared with pig grease. It was a lie used to stir up trouble against the English, and it nearly worked, because to the troops, pigs were unclean, anathema.

I smiled. "How nice of you, Major. Please, gentlemen, do be seated." And I took the chair closest to the hearth. There was a fire blazing there, and it felt good on a sunny but chill afternoon. "May I offer you tea?"

I rang the little bell on the table beside my chair, and we chatted for a few minutes, catching up on family news—his—and my travels, until Shanta brought in the tea tray. More time was spent on the polite formalities, and as soon as Harris and the Major had finished all the cakes on the tray, I felt I could ask what had brought them to Kent.

"You haven't come all this way just to see me, Harris. How can I be of service to you?"

Harris glanced at the Major and then said, "We have a problem. A young recruit. He has lied about his age and joined the Army. Because he's tall and his voice has already dropped, no one realized just how young he was until a Sergeant recognized his name and then reported the situation to the Major here."

"Recognized his name? Is he someone I know?"

It was the only reason I could think of for them to come here to me.

It was the Major who took up the story. "I'm not sure, ma'am. He lives with his grandfather. His parents are dead. It seems the grandfather never forgave his daughter for choosing to marry into the Army. I'm told he has made his grandson's life as wretched as he could, although surprisingly enough, he never neglected the lad's education. The circumstances were known to Sergeant Davis, who had served with the lad's father. The boy is filled with anger, and he's determined to join the Army, I think simply to spite his grandfather, rather than to follow in his father's footsteps." He coughed slightly, to hide his concern. "The question is, what do we do with him? He's too young to serve, you see. But sending him back to his grandfather is not a choice any of us who know the situation really care to make."

"Who, pray, is his grandfather?"

I don't know what I was expecting, but it was far from what I was about to hear!

"Marcus Sinclair. Do you know him, by any chance? It would help if you did."

I didn't. But I knew *of* him.

His father had had a title, but as a younger son, Marcus was merely an Honorable. Still, he married well, a young woman who came from another well-to-do family. They were apparently quite happy, had two children, a daughter and then a son. Marcus doted on the little girl. She was the image of her mother. When the son was born a few years later, the mother died of childbed fever, and the boy only survived her by a few days. Dorothea grew up to be both pretty and sweet, like her mother, and Marcus had high hopes for her. Instead, she eloped with an Army officer after he had angrily forbidden her to see him again.

That was where I came into the picture, because the young officer was in my late husband's Regiment. He wasn't as wealthy as Dorothea, he had no title, but he came from an old and very distinguished family—she had hardly married beneath her.

They had had a child, and when he was four, his parents were shot to death while they were posted to South Africa. Their killer was never found. It was in all the newspapers, an international tragedy. Their son was sent back to England with his Nanny, and handed over to the grandfather. End of a sad story. Or so we'd believed.

I said to the Major, "Shouldn't he be enrolled in a school somewhere? That would be the best solution to the problem."

"His grandfather didn't enroll him anywhere. Instead he brought in tutors."

I sighed. "What are we to do with him, then? Do we know anyone who could get him into Eton? Harrow?"

Harris spoke then. "That's where we hoped you could help us. He's officially enlisted, you see, and he's already halfway through his training. Glowing accounts from the Sergeants who have him in hand. Born soldier, like his father. But there's a great deal of anger in the lad, and he has some trouble with authority. If he's not court-martialed before he's shot for insubordination, I'll be surprised."

I thought he was exaggerating.

"Are you suggesting I should take a look at this young man?"

Relief on the faces of both officers. "It would be a kindness," Harris said.

Oh, dear.

"Very well. How do we go about this?"

They had thought this through. They had only waited for me to suggest the possibility of helping them.

"That shouldn't be at all difficult," Major MacInnes assured me. "He can be assigned to escort you to your meeting with me. That should give you an opportunity to inspect him."

"You'll stay the night, gentlemen, while I rearrange my trunks?"

They were willing to stay.

I ordered Shanta to prepare their rooms and asked my cook

to prepare a suitable dinner. He stared at me, then said, "I kill myself."

"There isn't time. Just do your best."

I left him to it.

IN THE MORNING, my carriage pulled up at the front door, my trunks, repacked overnight, were stowed in the boot, and the two officers joined me inside as Ram, my coachman, gave the horses the order to walk on.

The Regiment was headquartered in Hampshire. We arrived there two days later, having taken the train from Kent to London, where the Colonel, after a lovely dinner, bade me a warm goodbye.

Still, I had the feeling that he was beginning to wonder if he'd done the right thing by asking a civilian to help solve a military matter.

His carriage had just drawn up before my hotel, and I said rather bluntly, "Harris. Are you having second thoughts about my continuing my journey?"

He took my hand. "I met this young man—it was arranged by MacInnes, of course, quite by accident or so it appeared. It struck me afterward that if he returned to his home in Essex, either he would continue to try to enlist—or he would kill his grandfather. There is no other way out of his predicament."

I must admit. I was shocked. "How can you be so sure?"

Releasing my hand, he said, "I didn't wish to speak of this in front of the Major. But I remember Brandon's parents. Not well, of course. But the manner of their deaths stayed with me. Hugh was an up-and-coming officer, good reports and all that. Beginning to be noticed. His wife was such a lovely woman. But there was something about her, a strength perhaps, beneath her charm and lightness of heart. I did wonder if she had had a serious illness, a difficult recovery. Or looking back now, perhaps it was the break with her father. Who can say? I do recall being told after they were killed, and the child was to be carried back to England to his grandfather, that their Nanny pleaded with the police and Brandon's fellow officers not to send him to Essex. That when Lieutenant Brandon had been posted to South Africa, his wife had been adamant about accompanying him, refusing to remain in England without him, and neither parent would consider leaving the child with his grandfather. In the Nanny's hearing she had said at the time that she would rather see her child dead first. The Nanny was considered to be hysterical, she was dismissed, and Brandon's commanding officer found a family sailing to London from Cape Town. They were asked to take the child with them."

"That must have been extraordinarily difficult for him to understand. His parents dead, the only other familiar face taken away as well."

"Indeed. And from what I've gathered, no warm and loving welcome awaiting him in Essex, a house and a grandfather he did not know."

"Was the murderer ever caught?"

"A man was tried and hanged, yes."

"Does young Brandon have any financial resources?"

Harris was suddenly uncomfortable. I realized he'd spoken to the family's solicitors. "Hmm. He has no money of his own. There's a small allowance given him by his grandfather. While there is money in trust, he won't come into it until his thirtieth birthday. His grandmother's dowry. That had been his mother's, but she had never touched it. Instead she had put it in the child's name."

"A long wait until thirty."

"Yes."

"Why are you taking such an interest, Harris?"

"I don't know," he said after a moment. "Do you suppose I'm getting sentimental in my dotage?"

I laughed. "Or is it that he reminds you of someone? His father?" I could have bitten my tongue as I saw in the dim light of the carriage how his face changed. Trying to avoid anything painful, I added, "Then you think he might be as good a soldier?"

"I'm sorry that he can't wait. I believe Sandhurst would have taken him."

"Yes, well. One problem at a time."

"Quite."

We parted on good terms, as we always did. As I've mentioned, I've always been fond of Harris. And he of me. But I carried food for thought away with me.

FROM LONDON, ANOTHER train carried me to Lynford, and there my own carriage had arrived and was waiting to convey me to Regimental Headquarters.

I had to admit to a feeling of exhilaration and familiarity. I hadn't been back for some time, and secretly I had missed the orderly chaos of a post. After all, I'd spent much of my life both as a child and as a wife in places such as these. I had grown up to marry another officer in my father's Regiment, and we had been terribly happy—until I lost him to cholera at far too young an age . . .

Major MacInnes had gone ahead to prepare for my arrival, and as the carriage approached the gates, a young guard stepped out to ask my business. I told him with a smile that I'd been invited to take lunch with Major MacInnes.

After a glance at Ram, my majordomo and coachman, who was Indian, and immensely impressive in his turban and smart clothes, I was welcomed to Lynford and asked if I knew my way to the Major's quarters.

"I'm afraid not," I admitted, lying through my teeth.

"Let me summon someone to escort you."

He did, and in a few minutes, a tall young man in uniform came trotting to the gate, was told where to take me, and I asked him to join me in the carriage rather than sit with Ram on the box.

"Good morning," I said, "I hope I haven't taken you from something you'd rather be doing. But I'm glad of a guide."

"My pleasure, Mrs. Crawford," he said politely. He looked anything but pleased.

That was two of us lying through our teeth.

"And where are you from?" I asked, the epitome of a chatty elderly lady.

Grudgingly. "The North, ma'am."

Another lie.

"Are you indeed? Yorkshire? I'm not familiar with that part of the country. I live in Kent, you see. Ever been there, Private—er—"

"Private Brandon, ma'am. Will you please direct your coachman to take the first turning to his right and proceed to the brick building at the end of the road?"

"He understands perfect English," I said dryly. "Direct him yourself."

He flushed at that. "Thank you, ma'am." And raising his voice slightly, he told Ram where to go. I was interested to see he wasn't put off by an Indian servant. Although Ram would most certainly have taken offense at the term *servant*.

He had very strong views on his position in my household and the running thereof. I had occasionally had to remind him whose household it actually was.

"How long have you been in the Army, may I ask?"

"Four and a half months, ma'am." He was watching as Ram followed his directions, but taking his time about it—as he'd been instructed to do.

"And what made you decide to become a soldier?"

"The excitement of traveling, ma'am."

It was a ready answer, as if he'd used it often.

"Do you like it? Soldiering?"

"I can't answer that. So far, there's been nothing but training."

"You're a well-spoken young man. Have you considered becoming an officer?"

"No, ma'am. I am happy where I am."

Time to try a different tactic.

"I've been on a battlefield, Private Brandon. It's anything but exciting. In fact, it's quite terrifying and chaotic. Sometimes hard to tell friend from foe, and the smell of gunpowder and blood and the sweat of busy men is all you know as you struggle to stay alive by the end of the day."

He turned to stare at me. Dark hair, dark eyes. Good bones. His features hadn't fully formed at fourteen, but I thought he was going to become a rather handsome young man in due course. He was slim but filling out with his training, and if I was right, he was very likely going to be as tall as my late husband, over six feet. Good hands, well shaped, and a generous mouth, belying the anger I could sense in him. He was enduring training, I thought, eager to get on with the main event.

"When were you on a battlefield?" he challenged. Then, remembering his manners, "Ma'am?"

I could see, quite clearly, that he thought I was making it up. And so I told him the truth.

"In India, in the Great Sepoy Rebellion. It was a bloody time. I was only a child, but there was no sparing any child's sensibilities, when there was so much death all around. I have seen men with the most terrible wounds, and felt helpless to save them. I watched women weep over children dying of cholera, and children weeping over parents who died in the agonies of fever. It was an experience that haunts my dreams even now. But I think it made me stronger, more determined to survive. That has stood me in good stead for much of my life. It has not been an easy one, although it has had its moments."

I'd watched his eyes as I spoke.

He regarded me for a moment, and then he said, "I can't imagine going through that as a child. I'm sorry."

Surprised, I added, "Have you considered the fact that you could be wounded? Killed? We are presently at peace, of course, but there are still wars. In Sudan, against the Mahdi. That was a small war, but men died. Prisoners were tortured."

"I think I'm prepared for it, ma'am."

There was a tightness in his voice that I understood—he'd fought other battles that had left their own terrible scars. He'd been the scapegoat because his mother had disappointed her father, then failed to live long enough to be punished for it herself. Or to protect her child from what was to come. And instead of breaking under such treatment, he had endured.

I was beginning to understand something else. This boy—this man—had spent most of his life with adults around him. I doubted if he'd had playmates or friends his own age.

His grandfather, the household staff, the tutors. Not one of whom teased the child or romped with him across the lawns, hiding with him from those very tutors, begging Cook for treats. None of the things of childhood that made memories and brought joy.

Changing directions, I said, "Did you have a dog, as a child?"

"No, ma'am." It was curt, inviting no further questions. "I did have horses."

"I had a pet monkey, once. An orphan, then it grew up and ran off to join the others of its kind in the temple. My mother thought it a disgusting creature. She was just as glad to see the end of it. Of course I adored it, sitting on my shoulder as I walked about, making the ladies nervous for fear it might leap onto *their* shoulders at any moment."

He smiled suddenly, and I saw a very different side of him. The fourteen-year-old.

"There were kittens in the barn. A black male by the name of Dickens would follow me around outside, but he never ventured as far as the house."

Ram was drawing up outside Major MacInnes's quarters.

I said, "Thank you, Private Brandon, for making my journey less tedious."

"My pleasure, ma'am." Whether it was true or not, he was polite enough to say so.

I had listened carefully, and I'd heard little warmth in his voice. Except for that brief moment about the monkey. There was nothing personal in his coolness. Simply stated, it was suppressed anger that drove him. Clearly his grandfather had killed any outward display of emotions. And Simon had learned one lesson very well—that feelings were an easy way inside one's armor, a chink that invited unexpected attacks. And so he had hidden any of his so deep that no chinks appeared on the surface. Only the anger showed through.

"Good luck with your future. I hope we will meet again someday."

"Indeed, ma'am. Thank you."

He handed me from the carriage and escorted me to the door, passing me on to the Officer of the Day.

"Has it changed much?" the Major asked after warmly greeting me. "The post?"

"Not terribly. The young do look younger every year, however."

He laughed, offering me a chair and tea. I declined the tea, and he sat down across from me.

The laughter was gone now. We had other, more serious matters to attend to.

"What did you think of our young man? What are we to do with him?"

"I think he ought to become the soldier he wants so desperately to be."

Surprised, the Major looked at me.

"He's underage—"

"Yes, I know. But there are two reasons why he was able to get this far before anyone caught him. One is his size. The other is the fact that he's been surrounded by adults all his life, and he isn't a child in his mind. Perhaps hasn't been for a very long time. My guess is that he's more mature than some of the eighteen-year-olds who pass through your hands."

"That's an interesting observation," he said thoughtfully, but he was still frowning. "Would you send a child into battle?"

Instead of replying directly, I asked, "Is his grandfather searching for him? Does he want him back?"

"We've made discreet inquiries. Apparently he considers his grandson dead. He has not called in the police or made any search for the boy. And from what I gather, he never will. He isn't a man who easily bends."

"His grandson has learned that from him."

He cleared his throat. "I believe what the Colonel actually wanted was for you to take him off our hands. He can't stay in the Army, Mrs. Crawford. He can't go home. It's a waste to send a lad like that out into the world to fend for himself. There's value there, Mrs. Crawford. I see it, his Sergeant sees it. Brandon never complains, he's no slacker at anything asked of him and often outperforms those older than he is. Because of his physical abilities, he doesn't tire, fall behind, or fail. Give him several more years, and the Regiment would be very pleased to have him."

"I have no right to take him. I am not related to him. I have no legal authority to become his guardian."

"Do you think that's required? In this case?"

"We are a household of women, except for a temperamental cook, and Ram, my majordomo. He will resent that, and he will run away and enlist somewhere else. Scotland, Wales—and if he's found out, he'll try yet again. Surely you see that. And I cannot force him to return to my house, even if I find him."

He sighed. "Yes. I do see it. I know myself I'd chafe in his place and be angrier still. But what can we do? He isn't of legal age to make his own decisions. We shall have no choice but to return him to his grandfather."

"I shudder to think how he will be received in that house. It will only make him more determined to go as soon as someone's back is turned."

"I don't believe he's been physically abused—beaten—" the Major began, but I cut across his words.

"I doubt his grandfather would have him beaten. But there are other abuses—mental anguish and withholding of warmth or love—that can bring just as much pain as physical blows. And I have a feeling his grandfather knows how to wield those with energy and passion."

"The anger? Yes. I'm told he didn't fight back—he simply endured—waited to leave as soon as he could." He shook his head. "The Colonel will be as disappointed as I am that we haven't a solution. You've made this journey for nothing."

"Not quite nothing." I had already thought of an answer. But the Army is the Army and doesn't take lightly to change of any kind.

"How does he get along with the other recruits? The other Sergeants, whom I expect don't know the truth about him?"

Wary, Major MacInnes said, "Well enough. He won't take anything from anyone, and he pursues his training with determination." He added as if forced to be truthful, "There are no complaints on his record. He has been in several fights. In each case he was provoked, and then gave a good account of himself. He accepted his punishment without objections." He played with a button on the sleeve of his uniform, and I waited.

"The odd thing is, I believe he's bent all his will toward proving himself. He wants this very badly, and that compels him to succeed. He will do his best not to make any mistakes, because they could cost him what he wants. What's more, he's better educated than most recruits, and this helps him learn faster. In someone older, I'd call this determination admirable. In fact, the makings of a remarkable officer someday. In Brandon, it's rather sad to see such dedication wasted."

"Then I suggest we let him complete it. His training."

"But to what purpose? It will be several more years before he's old enough to serve. And he's a child among rough men."

"You just told me he gave a good account of himself."

"Their language—their stories—these aren't fit for his ears."

"Major. Did you have older brothers?"

"I—yes, but I don't see—"

"I would imagine that at twelve you could swear like a stable boy if put to it. And it did no lasting harm to your family's expectations for you."

He had the grace to blush. "That's not the same."

"Oh, I agree. But a bootblack at a hotel has no such protection from the vulgar in life. His family is his wits. He has to grow up quickly if he's to survive. I think we ought to find out just what this young man is made of. Who knows? We might be pleasantly surprised. Then we can decide what should be done about him."

"I don't see—the Army isn't—and this isn't fair to Brandon."

"I think giving him a chance to prove himself is immensely fair. The last thing we wish to do is break his spirit. His grandfather couldn't, and it would be wrong of us to break him in the name of Regulations. Keep an eye on him. Find something to do with him when he ought to be on leave. Some course or other, that won't smack of favoritism. Or punishment. That's where the danger to his safety will lie. The first drunken brawl in a pub, and the truth will come out."

"He doesn't appear to gravitate toward that sort of crowd."

"I'm glad to hear it. But there will be women who are eager to provide an education in other directions. Syphilis has been the downfall of many a promising soldier."

He flushed a little at my plain speaking. "I've no doubt."

"*Could* young Brandon complete his training, if he were allowed?"

"It's highly irregular. If we'd never known, of course, he might well have completed it."

"He might well fail, solving the problem for us."

MacInnes shook his head. "What if he doesn't?"

I rose. "Keep me informed of his progress. Then I will see to his future."

Not certain whether he was relieved or not, the Major smiled. "Thank you."

"Not at all. Now, what about that luncheon you promised me?"

IT *WAS* IRREGULAR, I had to agree, I thought, traveling back to Kent. But I'd taken to young Brandon. I wanted to see whether he could finish what he'd started. I'd been a part of the Army most of my life, I probably knew more about how it worked than the Major, and possibly more than Harris. There had been many cases of boys passing themselves off as old enough to enlist. Some had been caught, others hadn't. And telling the Major that I would take over had been all he needed to hear to humor me now.

OVER THE WEEKS ahead, I received regular reports on young Brandon's progress, and much to the Major's dismay—I could read that between the lines—the boy had done everything that was asked of him. And when I returned to the Regiment and met him again, even I was surprised at what I found.

He had filled out—I was sure he'd grown another inch taller—and he was quite proud, in a quiet way, of what he'd accomplished. And I think he realized for the first time that he had worth. That he had earned something his grandfather could never diminish or take from him.

I was rather pleased that he remembered me. "Good morning, Mrs. Crawford," he'd greeted me. "I believe you know your way?"

"I do." I'd told Ram to tell the Duty Officer that he needed an escort. And the Major had arranged for him to be available. "But I miss my days here. Sit with me and tell me what you thought of the training. How did you fare?"

"Well enough, I expect. I'm looking forward to joining the Regiment. It's presently in India, I believe."

"Yes, so I've been told," I replied affably. "A cousin of mine is a Captain out there."

His ears pricked up. "Indeed?" But he didn't ask for an introduction, which I found very interesting. He wanted to make even that step on his own merit.

"Traveling out there is easier than it was in my parents' day. Still, it's a long way from home."

"I don't have any close ties here. Unlike some of the men, who are married. It will be easier for me."

"Any young woman in your future?"

"Not at present, ma'am."

"And here we are. At the Major's office. How are you at languages, young man? India has more than its share. I learned them as a child, like a sponge, soaking them up from servants and villagers. But I understand they can be difficult for many people, and the written language has no Western alphabet to help one."

"I was taught French, and found it easy enough."

It was the only time he'd spoken of his past. "That's a good start," I agreed, as he turned me over to my escort at the Major's quarters. "The very best of luck, Private Brandon."

MAJOR MACINNES WAS—TO put it mildly—delighted to see me.

"I've kept my part of the bargain," he said. "I'm eager to hear what you will do with our young man."

"He's finished his training? Sergeant Davis is satisfied with his progress?"

"He appears to be quite satisfied. I don't believe he expected Brandon to finish. And I have a feeling, knowing the Sergeant, that he never stinted his training. If anything, he pushed Brandon just a bit harder than he pushed any other recruit in his charge."

"I'm glad to hear that. And I've spoken to Harris—the Colonel—on my way through London. He's agreed to my suggestion." I neglected to mention that I'd had to persuade him to consider my point of view. "I have a cousin out in India, an officer in the Regiment. Up in the North-West Frontier. They're sending five casualties home to England, and they've requested five men to replace them. Young Brandon will be one of them."

The Major stared at me, openmouthed, then snapped it shut as he realized how he must look. "This is highly irregular—" he began.

"Well, I've known Richard Crawford all of his life. I think he's the perfect choice to take this young man and find out just what he's made of."

"Major Crawford?"

I raised my eyebrows.

"I happened to see the list of promotions. He's just been given his majority.'

"Even better," I agreed. "Then you'll arrange that Private Brandon is on that ship to India?"

"I don't see that I have much choice. If Colonel Clifford has agreed. But I can't think—it's a huge step from training in the safety of England and sending a boy out where fighting is common."

I smiled. "It isn't the end of the world, Major. He may turn out to be an excellent soldier. And if he doesn't, we can all profess surprise that he is underage."

"I expect that will not be the best defense at a court martial," he said dryly.

I smiled. "There are two matters I must put to you, from Colonel Clifford. First is, as I understand it, there are only four people who know that Brandon is underage. It will remain among the four of us. No one else will be told. And no mention will be made of his past. He's just a young man from Essex—or Yorkshire—or wherever he claims to have come from, who wants to be a soldier. It will not help him succeed if he realizes he's an object of either curiosity or pity."

"Not even Major Crawford or his superiors should be told?"

"No. Let's give Brandon a chance to show his talents. Or lack thereof. Harris—Colonel Clifford agrees with me that he should be treated just like any other soldier. Nothing from his past should follow him. We are also agreed there?"

"Again, I appear not to have much choice."

He was a little uneasy. But, of course, by the time lunch was over, I had him supporting the suggestion as if it were his own brilliant idea.

Just as Colonel Clifford had agreed with me by the time we'd finished dinner. Men are always more amenable after a good meal and a little wine.

WHAT NO ONE knew was that I wrote to Richard out in India. As soon as I was back in Kent. After congratulating him on his promotion, I went on:

The Regiment is sending you the five men I've been told you requested to complete your roster. One of them I wish to call to your attention, dear Richard. He's too young to be a soldier. But he's completed his training with honor. Keep an eye on him, if you please, and keep me informed of his progress. He doesn't know that I have taken an interest in him. Best to keep it that way. But I'm a fairly good judge of men. I must tell you that he's carrying a heavy burden of anger with him. Still, his father was a fine soldier, an officer, and while Brandon doesn't wish to go that direction, in time he might. Give my love to little Bess. I do miss her so! And love to Clarissa as well. Please tell her I am sending some new books out to her shortly. And know you are always dear to my heart.

own. But he stood his ground where he could, and kept her out of trouble. Well, most of the time. I was sometimes hard-pressed to keep a straight face.

He'd been here two months when my batman retired and re-turned to England. I offered Brandon that position, and to my surprise, he turned it down.

"If it's all the same to you, sir, I don't want to be a servant."

seldom have any trouble dressing myself in the mornings putting myself to bed at night," I told him dryly. "I want ne around my family who is capable of doing what is asked but who is there when I am not, to keep them safe."

ught he was about to turn me down a second time.

"I'll assign someone else to trail around after my daughter."

surprise, he smiled and said, "I don't object to that, sir. mp—begging your pardon, sir—but I like her."

ready adored him. I thought primarily because she could manipulate him into letting her have her way, he couldn't, she liked him all the more. She'd told hat Brandon reminded her of me. That was rather a e I had found myself thinking that he was more like er had.

nda apprised of all these happenings—my letters to sound like diaries of my days.

finally. "This position. It's yours, if you want it. ose Private Williams."

that. "I don't think he's the right man. Sir."

But when I quietly looked into the matter, I Williams was something of a gossip, and that of the running.

I didn't add that I wished I, too, were traveling to India this autumn. My heart was buried out there in the heat and dust and monsoon rains. I remember that day as if it were yesterday, standing there watching the coffin slipping into the dusty earth, surrounded by women in black and men in the dress uniforms of the Regiment. My husband was buried in his, a lock of my hair in his pocket.

Very irregular, of course. But only he and I knew . . .

It was thick and dark, then, and he loved it so. He has never grown old in my heart.

Richard

India, 1900

I READ MELINDA's letter with some dismay. India just now—this part of it at least—was no place for a raw young soldier. I'd requested men with some experience, and the other four were just that.

When the five arrived, I was out on patrol, and they were settled in the barracks by the time I returned.

And young Brandon had already been in his first fight. When I summoned him to the bungalow after dinner and asked him to give an account of himself, he surprised me by saying, "It was not unexpected. Sir."

"What do you mean by that?"

"On the crossing from England, the four men with me had made fun of my accent, the fact that I'd never been out of the country before—the usual. I finally had to stand my ground, sir. Or I'd never have had the respect of a single man here."

I said, "Indeed." He had a good point.

I'm not sure just what I'd expected after reading M[elinda's] note—some slim, quiet boy who might last a month out[...] gardless of his excellent training record.

I should have known better. Melinda had spent m[...] with the Army.

Standing before me was a broad-shouldered, ne[...] young man, who was still growing. I don't know [...] of India or what India would think of him, b[...] discover he appeared to be a soldier and that h[im]self without my protection.

I sent Brandon on his way, thinking th[...] it. Two days later, he was back on the ca[...] nature of the fight this time.

"He was abusing a horse, sir. Ther[...]

When I looked further into the [...] was absolutely correct.

I began to keep my eye on Pr[...] scrapes he got into, he was u[...] gument. But I wanted to get [...] was surprisingly level-head[...] Better educated than mos[...] class than most private s[...] good at languages, bec[...] remarkable ease and [...] proper accents, a gif[...]

For a time—be[...] daughter, Bess, [...] hope that she [...] sent with her [...] of leading him [...]

In the end, Brandon agreed to be my batman, and it kept him out of trouble while I found it increasingly pleasant to have him around.

There was still a strong thread of anger in him. I had a feeling it would be some years before that faded. What's more, he seemed to thrive on challenges as if eager to test himself. And he was very good at every task I set for him. Eventually, he became one of the best scouts for the cantonment. He could trail a horse across rock and slip in and out of an enemy camp with impunity. At the same time, he never took foolish risks, often one of the difficulties with young, inexperienced men out for glory. The reports I got from the Sergeants were judiciously approving. And when I was in the field with him, I saw the same restraint. Nor did anyone question his courage.

My wife scolded me for putting him in such danger.

"If anything happens to him," she said, "Bess will be broken-hearted. Besides, I rather like him myself. When I go to the markets, it's nice to have him with me. One look at him, and no one troubles me. Do you know, I think he's going to be as tall as you are?"

"My darling girl," I told her, "Brandon's a soldier, not a lapdog."

"You have plenty of soldiers to push around as you please. It's unfair of you to take Brandon as well."

The upshot of *that* was we never spoke, Brandon and I, about any risks we were called upon to take. It seemed the easiest way out of the matter. I've faced howling tribesmen intent on killing me, and kept my head. It was far more difficult to argue with my wife and daughter.

But skirmishes were a way of life out here. Simon showed just how fine a soldier he would be, and early on, I saw in him what Melinda must have seen. A good man in a fight, steady head, steady aim. Although how she knew Simon Brandon I had no idea. He never spoke of her, and anyone who had met her always found something to say about Cousin Melinda. I asked her once in a letter if she'd been party to sending him out here, one of those five replacements. But she told me that Colonel Clifford had brought him up in conversation because she had lived in India. That left me in the dark more than ever.

Bess was soon old enough to learn to shoot, and I left that to Simon. He'd already quietly improved her riding. She preferred full tilt, until he'd explained that it was unfair to the horse. Now she rode well and was often out with him when he was off duty. But he also made certain she never escaped her governess for too long. And I sometimes overheard him asking her about her studies, as if he were her elder brother.

Meanwhile, Clarissa had become quite good friends with the Maharani, whose lands were adjacent to the cantonment, and we were often invited to the palace. On occasion she also came to dine with us. She had a lovely young daughter of sixteen, and Bess sometimes accompanied Clarissa to the Palace, under the watchful eye of Brandon or one of the other trustworthy men.

Parvati had been betrothed to the son of a Rajah since she was twelve. Clarissa was worried that she had been brought up with more freedom than was common in girls her age and would find marriage into a more conservative Princely family difficult. But when the time came, she seemed to be looking forward to managing her own household. Bess however moped for a week after Parvati left for her new home.

It's a very different life out here on the North-West Frontier. Hot—dry. We're more likely to see camels than elephants, although the Maharani keeps two for feast days. And we are never safe. The compound has been attacked seven times since I've been out here. Which is why Clarissa and Bess can defend themselves.

Three years after young Brandon arrived, there was a particularly nasty fight near the Khyber Pass. We lost two men, and we would have lost more, if it hadn't been for him. He brought our Sergeant and two Privates back under heavy fire, and kept the tribesmen at bay until reinforcements could reach them. When we got back to the compound, Sergeant Lester asked to see me after he'd been patched up.

"How are you feeling?" I asked when he stepped into my office. He was still rather pale, and one of his bandages still showed bright blood.

"Well enough, sir."

"Do you or Benson or Williams need time off?"

"No, sir. They've given us a day at the Infirmary. That'll do." He shifted a little. "It's not for that I've come, sir. What Private Brandon did today showed initiative and more than a little courage. I've been thinking he's ready for a promotion."

I picked up my pen so that he wouldn't see my reaction. "He's—inexperienced, still." I'd almost said *young*.

"Yes, sir, I understand. But he's got his head on straight. Never ruffled. Reminds me a little of you, when you first joined the Regiment."

I cleared my throat. "Um. I shall certainly take this suggestion under advisement."

Sergeant Lester regarded me for a moment, then said, "Do you feel that such a recommendation is unwarranted, sir?"

Forced to be honest, I had to tell him, "Oh, I agree. But he's still rather new to India, don't you think?"

"Begging your pardon, sir, but I think because he's been your batman, you haven't realized how much he's changed since his arrival. He's good at tactics, sir, far more so than Corporal Hayes. Unlike Corporal Taylor, he's picked up the native tongues, and he's brought us gossip from the bazaars that's been damned useful."

But Simon Brandon wasn't yet old enough to be a soldier at all. It had taken me some time to realize this. Bess was reading a book that Melinda had sent out for her birthday, and Simon, seeing the title, said, "It's quite good, I read it when I was thirteen." But that particular book had not been published then. Simon was not a liar—therefore he wasn't twenty, he must barely be seventeen!

Had Melinda known this? Was it why she had asked me to keep an eye on that particular recruit? I began to watch him, but he was damned good at concealing the truth. I could never be quite sure . . .

I was obligated to report my suspicions straightaway. And I found I couldn't. For his sake, and my own.

The Sergeant was waiting for my answer.

"I agree, Sergeant. Still, let's wait and see, shall we?"

It was dismissal. Lester was clearly unhappy about my refusal to agree with him, but I hadn't even told Clarissa what I knew about Brandon. Although, being Clarissa, she had seen things in that young man that even I hadn't. And I had to admit to myself that there was a personal interest. We'd lost a son, Clarissa and I. I'd like to think that, if he'd lived, he'd have been rather like Brandon. I wondered, sometimes, if she felt the same. I hadn't asked her. James was too sensitive a subject to bring up even between ourselves.

And so I hadn't mentioned Lester's visit to her.

Christmas that year was to be a special time. The Maharani was planning to mark the anniversary of her husband's death, and

Melinda was coming out to visit. We were looking forward to her arrival, but when there was an attack on a friendly tribe, we had to race to their aid.

Neither Simon nor I got back to the cantonment in time to take part in any of the festivities. In fact, I missed Melinda's visit altogether. She had moved on to Delhi and other places where she had friends among the Army, the Government, and the native princes. But it was apparent that she and Clarissa had had long conversations.

We were dressing for dinner on Twelfth Night, when Clarissa said, "Have you ever talked to Melinda about Simon?"

"Yes. Since Colonel Clifford had discussed posting him to India with her, she had asked me to let her know how he was faring."

"Hmmm," she said.

I turned to look at her. "What? My shirt? My shoes?"

Smiling, she said, "Of course not. I couldn't help but wonder—I think Melinda was rather disappointed that she had to leave before you returned."

Teasing her, I said, "I'm not surprised. Rumor has it I'm her favorite male cousin."

"You're her only male cousin, and you know it. Still. I had the odd feeling that she'd hoped to see Simon."

"It's possible that Colonel Clifford had asked her to let him know how his young private had fared."

"She and Sergeant Lester went riding several times."

I'd left Lester and a few other seasoned men to keep an eye on our flank, as it were, because we weren't certain when we left that the attack on the friendly tribe wasn't a feint to disguise a different target altogether. Lester hadn't been happy about staying behind, but he was very popular with the troops and I trusted him to make the right decisions if the time came. He was seven years from retirement, but I'd heard him say repeatedly that he'd retire in his coffin. The word *experienced* was minted for him.

"Did they indeed?" My cousin Melinda had an unerring ability to choose the best person to question, if there was information she wanted. "And what did she and Lester have in common?"

"I don't know," she said, turning around so that I could fasten her pearls and as always, kiss the small curls on the charming back of her neck. "I had the oddest feeling that she was subtly asking about Simon. I know for a fact she and Bess talked about him several times."

I smiled. "Bess adores him. Of course she talks about him. All the time."

Turning back to me, she said, "And that's another subject. Is she growing too fond of him?"

"Fond? She treats him like her horse or dog or kitten. I've heard her telling him what to do in any given circumstance and how to go about it. She knows how to get her way. I've often been amused by the problems he's faced dealing with our sweet daughter."

Clarissa laughed. "Yes, true enough. But Simon has benefited from that responsibility too, you know. Bess has drawn out a different side of him, settled and more relaxed. But back to Melinda. Do you think she might know his family? I have never—never, Richard!— heard him speak of any family. Mother, father, grandparent—it's as if he was born in a teacup, and has no one."

"Does that bother you, my dear?" I was earnest about that, but tried to ask it lightly.

"No. He has lovely manners—he's been brought up well. Educated, although he doesn't talk about it. It's just—I have seen him sometimes look sad when you and Bess and I are playing a game or disagreeing with each other—small family things that must touch some chord with him, and yet he has never said so much as 'It's my mother's birthday,' or 'My father was a solicitor.' The sort of thing people will do when they've had a happy youth."

"Perhaps it was too happy—and something happened."

Clarissa frowned. "Is that it? I'd like very much to think so. I've thought, sometimes too, that he's been the happiest in a long time, out here. Not in the beginning. He was too angry to feel anything else. But that's slowly changed in the last year or so. You've been a very good influence on him. Perhaps that's what Melinda had in mind, when she agreed with Colonel Clifford that India was the right choice for him." She hunted for a fan, and finding it, added, "When Melinda cares for someone, she is as ferocious as a tiger fighting for her cub. Take young Rutledge, for example. She's been a very good influence on him."

"She sees him often. I don't know that she's ever seen Simon."

Clarissa said, as the dinner gong went, "I expect she has. If only from a distance. He's a strange young man. But I've grown quite fond of him too."

IN THE NEW year, I had a friend in London look up Brandon's father, to see if he had a military record. I was curious to see if there was some problem there that might explain why the son had enlisted rather than applying to Sandhurst. It would have been easier if I'd asked Melinda. I've no doubt she could contrive to find out anything from the Army—she knows everyone who had ever kept a secret. But if she could pretend not to know anything about our young man, it was best if I found my own sources.

The response was a long time in coming. And it made interesting reading.

Brandon's paternal great-grandfather had been in the Guards, a good officer and a good soldier. Not always the same thing. His paternal grandfather had never been well enough to go into the Army, but apparently he'd encouraged Brandon's father to follow the family tradition. Hugh went to Sandhurst, but preferred a line regiment to the Guards, having little taste for their ceremonial duties. He'd proven himself to be someone to watch, adept at languages, a good tactician, and quite popular with his men. He saw to their welfare and the families who had come out with the Army. Promotion is slow in times of peace, but Hugh was being considered for one when he and his wife were ambushed on the drive home from a regimental affair. Neither survived the attack, leaving a small child who was sent back to his family in England.

Nothing in that to raise an eyebrow. Except when one did the arithmetic and discovered that our soldier was indeed not only as young in years as Melinda had indicated, he was younger.

And how the devil had she known that?

Perhaps a more important question was, why was Brandon allowed to continue his training?

I'd have wagered a year's pay that Melinda had had a hand in that. For some reason, she had sent Brandon out to me, where he could succeed or fail on his own merit.

Why had he enlisted? Why hadn't he waited until he was a few years older and could go to Sandhurst?

Clarissa was right. He never spoke of his family or reminisced about his childhood. No mention of his first pony or a favorite dog or a holiday taken with cousins or friends from school. Either he was orphaned a second time by whichever family member he'd been sent home to, or he had not liked them, to the point of running away to enlist as a common soldier as soon as he could pass, physically, the age requirement. I had the feeling it was the latter—that would explain the deep anger in him, the determination not to fail in his chosen profession, and his silence.

My first thought was to tell Clarissa what I'd learned. And then I decided against that, for the simple reason that these were Simon's secrets I'd uncovered, and I had no right to pass them on.

On what would have been his actual eighteenth birthday, he was promoted to Corporal. And he accepted that promotion with a sudden shyness, as if he hadn't expected it.

A popular decision with the men, of course. I stood there watching them pound him on the back, offering to stand him a drink, and eager to begin the celebration, out of view of the officers.

The Colonel, standing beside me, rubbed his chin, then said, "He's an unusual lad. You've done well by him, Crawford."

"The material was there to work with."

"Have you suggested that he might return to England and apply to Sandhurst? I think he's got the makings of a good officer."

Silently hoping to hell that they didn't get Simon too drunk or into any other trouble as I watched them cross the parade ground in a rowdy group, I said, "I haven't mentioned it, sir. Should I?"

And had to admit to myself that if Corporal Brandon left for England, I would sorely miss him. On the heels of that thought, I tried to imagine what I would tell Clarissa. Or—God forfend!— how I could explain his going to Bess.

The Colonel considered the question for a moment, then said, "Let's see how he handles his new rank. What sort of officer he might make. Then we'll know if that's the right decision or not. But the Army will have a place for a man like that. And I'd be happy to sign the papers for him, when the time comes."

I waited a year, watched as he'd taken his new authority to

heart, and after dinner at the house one evening, I put the question to him. Clarissa had left the table to send Bess to bed. We were alone with the port.

I had no choice, really. He'd earned it, and it would have been derelict of me as an officer and a man not to give him the chance he deserved.

His response surprised me.

"Thank you, sir, for the offer. But I'm satisfied where I am. I'd rather stay, if you don't mind."

"You've earned the right to decide your future. It would mean more money, more authority, more social position. You'd be giving the orders, not taking them. And I must be honest, Simon. I think you should take this opportunity. It could change your entire life in ways you may not yet understand."

"Then you'd rather I leave." His gaze was steady on my face, and I couldn't read what he was thinking.

I looked for the right response. "It has nothing to do with what I'd like. I have certain duties as an officer. Among them is to do what is best for the men under me. If you tell me you would like to return to England, you'll go with my blessing and my letter approving the change in your rank. If you stay here, I will not think less of you for turning this chance down." I smiled, to take some of the tension out of the air. "God knows what Bess will say if you go, but I outrank her. Barely."

He smiled then, as I'd hoped he would.

"Then I'll stay, sir."

"Will you tell me, if at any stage you change your mind? I can make the necessary arrangements at any point in your career. You should know that."

"I'm not likely to change my mind, sir. But thank you for asking me. I appreciate that more than I can say."

Because his father had been to Sandhurst? I thought that might be behind his gratitude. But sometimes I'm wrong.

Years later, I understood that what he'd found in India was a home he'd wanted for a very long time, and the family he couldn't remember but had yearned for over ten tormented years.

In 1910 his world—and ours—suddenly turned upside down.

And I had had to watch the hands of the clock move slowly but inexorably toward dawn, and his hanging.

Clarissa

THE ODD THING was, I'd liked Simon from the start. He reminded me of Richard and the stories I'd heard about him at Simon's age. That threshold between boy and man when ideals and growing pains clash. But Richard had had a very happy upbringing. There wasn't that undercurrent in him that I very quickly saw in Simon.

I'd been the one who had suggested to Richard that Simon take over the duties of protecting Bess.

Out here, the dangers were quite real. I had no illusions about that—I'd seen the dead brought in. Orders kept the women and children on the grounds of the cantonment most of the time, but when one of us—officers' wives or wives of the ranks—had to leave the compound, we were escorted. And none of us raised objections. We understood why. The largest or most experienced man was usually our escort.

Bess had just turned five, precocious and spirited. It had occurred to me that perhaps her youthful enthusiasm for life might be just the thing to help Simon find his own feet out here, and possibly lessen some of the anger in him.

Richard had said to me privately after he'd first brought Simon home as his batman, "He's going to make a good soldier—if he isn't shot first for insubordination. Do what you can with him, love. Between us we might succeed in saving him for the Regiment."

I'd laughed, but I knew precisely what he was asking. I'd married the Army along with Richard, and I knew just how it worked.

Pairing Simon with Bess had proved to be a stroke of genius. I had the feeling that he hadn't been brought up with brothers or sisters or even cousins. He didn't understand her teasing at first, or her attempts to wheedle him into allowing her to have her way. But he was quick to learn! The change in both of them in six months' time was remarkable. Bess was less accustomed to having her own way, less headstrong. And he'd learned to laugh with her. What's more, it was far more successful than assigning one of the older Sergeants to ride with her or go into the bazaar with her. She had most of our Indian staff under her thumb—she'd learned to speak Hindi like a native from them, and Urdu from the outside staff and our gatekeeper, whose task it was to see that no one entered the compound without permission.

I worried a little that she adored Simon quite so much. Soldiers were killed, invalided home, transferred. And she was only a child, and a very warmhearted little girl who saved spiders and crickets our housekeeper chased with a vengeance and a broom. She rescued wounded birds and did what she could for the wild dogs. I was grateful that we had a veterinarian for the horses, because she took him her patients and helped care for them as they healed.

He'd complained at first. Insisting that birds were not his concern. I didn't need to ask Richard to intervene on behalf of the beleaguered veterinarian, because Bess soon had the man under her thumb as well. Still, I drew the line at the snake she wanted to bring home, and in the end Dr. Winters kept it in a wicker cage in the stables until it could be released. I was never sure what had made the snake ill, but I *was* fully prepared to hold a funeral for it in a corner of the compound that Bess had insisted we set aside for the patients that sadly hadn't survived.

Bess first met the Maharani when she'd had her last child. Bess was three then and wanted to bring the baby back with us. That had charmed the Maharani, and she'd insisted that I bring Bess with me whenever I visited after that.

Bess treated the little Prince as if he were her pet, and it was sweet to see the two of them playing together. The difference in station never occurred to her, and as he learned to walk, she led him about the Palace, showing him everything that she herself found interesting, from the elephants to the kitchens. The cooks always had something for them, little cakes, a sweet dumpling boiled in syrup spiced with cinnamon and nutmeg, or dates with almond centers and rolled in brown sugar. They returned to the nursery covered in sticky things, while the child's bodyguard professed to know nothing about what they might have got into. The Maharani turned an indulgently blind eye.

"He'll be leaving for school in England soon enough. I want him to remember his home as a happy place," she told me.

"Not until he's nine or ten," I protested. "Surely."

She sighed. "In my great-grandfather's day, he ruled. Now I acquiesce. The Governor-General wishes our young Princes to be educated in England. But let's not look ahead. It will be here soon enough." And she sent for music to cheer us.

Of course, it was good politically to stay on terms with the nearby Indian Princes. But I liked the Maharani for herself, not because it was expedient. Their power had been reduced considerably, as the Maharani had pointed out. And sadly, the sons sent to England to learn to rule wisely were introduced as well to Society—Ascot, Biarritz, the pleasures of Paris—preferring these to returning home. All the while the winds of change were blowing ever stronger, and even the sources of their wealth were quietly drying up.

The Maharani cared about her people, and they still looked to her for guidance. Often she helped where the Government and the Army could do little. Richard had said to me privately that in another generation, the Princes would be little more than empty titles—if they were allowed to keep those.

How sad for the little boy running after Bess on the short, fat legs of babyhood, seeing only the pretty things all around him, the enormous white tusks on either side of the ornate gold throne, the ropes of pearls around his mother's neck, and gardens full of birds and glorious roses. His squeals of joy and sweet laughter as the cool water in the fountains splashed over his hands and face were precious.

Simon often accompanied me on these visits, after he became Richard's batman. It was amazing the gossip he gleaned from the guards and servants while he waited patiently in the Palace grounds. Richard found it very useful, because sometimes the servants knew things long before their employers did.

The same was true in the bazaars. While the box wallah dealt with my packages, Simon listened to the talk around us, taking the temperature of the villages in a way. He would sometimes steer me on a different path or to a different door, murmuring only, "It's best if we go this way, ma'am," or "I think today we might choose this shop instead." And I heeded his warnings. It saved face, for the Army. Officially, smuggling and other wrongdoing had been stamped out, but people don't change as quickly as laws. The Maharani's officials would quietly deal with such civilian problems, while the Army remained officially unaware of them. It was a system that worked amazingly well.

As Simon became more and more a part of our family, we had to be careful, Richard and I, not to appear to show any partiality for him. There were other men here with skills and abilities, and they had to be treated in exactly the same way. Fortunately, he was popular with the ranks, and that went a long way toward mitigating any ill will.

It was like having a son underfoot. Both painful and a pleasure for me. I made sure to treat him like the soldier he was, rather than the frustrated boy who tried to show Bess how to play tennis in the garden. Because I *could* see the boy in him, slowly emerging from the frigid hold he kept on his emotions. I never spoke of this to Richard. But sometimes, sitting on the veranda, listening to the shouts and laughter and loud quarrels, I thought how wonderful it would have been for Bess to have grown up with a brother. We had tended to spoil her, and it was good for her to play with other children in the cantonment, to take her turn at games, to share her toys, and not be among adults most of her day. But Simon gave her something else—as he kept an unobtrusive eye on her well-being, her safety, and her manners, he'd also tell her there and then, in no uncertain terms, how she'd transgressed. The older

men assigned to watch over her were gruff, showing their displea-
sure in offended silence. And because if she were too naughty, she
lost the privilege of his company, she would argue to show her
independence—then take Simon's advice. I found it amusing to
watch.

I quietly worried when Richard went on patrol or rode out to
deal with a problem among the tribes, which could easily end in
bloodshed. Now I found myself worrying about both of them. I
asked Simon once as we were walking through the bazaar, if he
had any family in England.

"No, ma'am. I don't."

"How sad," I'd answered, thinking how proud his parents
might be, or cousins or aunts. Most of our men had families back
in England.

"Not really, ma'am. It's easier. Not having to worry about *them*,
you see. Only myself."

"Are your parents dead, then?"

"When I was small. I find it difficult to remember them now. I
had a photograph of them for many years. It's gone now."

"How sad to lose something so precious."

But he didn't respond. I was to learn much, much later that it
was found among his things when he landed in Southampton and
taken away. I never learned by whom.

I was the one who had to tell Simon that his romantic feelings
for the Maharani's daughter could go nowhere.

Parvati was pretty, vivacious, and sixteen. She and Bess would
play shuttlecock or croquet on the lawns while Simon watched,
and sometimes the two girls would sit on the veranda together
as Parvati learned to play the sitar, laughing at Bess's attempts to
copy her.

It wasn't surprising that he should have been attracted to her.

"She's been betrothed since she was small. It's how things are done here," I told him gently. "The marriage will take place next year. And because we're not a part of that family, there's nothing we can do to prevent it."

"Does she love him?" he'd asked.

"I believe she's met him several times. It's like the royal family at home, Simon. Arrangements are made almost when a child is born, sometimes. Not that it always works out that way," I added, trying to be fair. "Queen Victoria for instance, had to marry someone the Government felt was suitable. As it turned out, this became a love match. But that's a matter of luck, I should think. And she was quite lucky."

He frowned. "Were you in love with the Major?"

It was a personal question that he shouldn't have asked. But I smiled and said, "I was. We met quite by accident, you know. I had come to London to meet a friend from school. And he was visiting her older brother. I've often thought that if I hadn't accepted Marion's invitation, I might well have fallen in love with someone else entirely."

"You don't really believe that!"

"I do. If I hadn't met the Major, I would have gone on with my life and in time met someone else I could love. Never knowing, of course, that there had been another choice."

"Would it have been the same?"

I'd shrugged. "Who knows? But since I did meet the Major, it all becomes a little silly to dwell on."

"What if he'd been in love with someone else, when you met?"

"Ah. I don't know. I expect I'd have had no choice but to walk away. However hard it would have been. You can't force someone to love you."

"No."

He'd taken it hard, because the girl was lovely and sweet natured, and they were both young, when it hurts so terribly much. I could only hope that she hadn't been aware of how he felt. I trusted Simon not to overstep his place, but she might have come to care without any attempt on his part.

I added, "If you let her know how much you care—and she feels the same toward you, you will only make it harder for her to marry as her family wishes. It will be painful to walk away. But it will be the greatest kindness you can offer her. You will leave her free to believe she loves the man she marries."

"I'd never thought of it in that way." But I saw the sadness in his eyes. "I'd had a feeling she might care for me."

"Shall I have someone else go with us to the Palace for a while?"

He took a deep breath. "For a few days?"

"Easily managed."

It was Bess who was upset that he wasn't with us on that Thursday when we went to the Palace for tea with the Maharani.

"He has duties besides riding with you and me," I told her. "We can't interfere with those. The Army needs him occasionally, you know."

But she hadn't smiled. She'd only nodded.

I never told her why he wasn't with us for the next fortnight. Or how he felt toward the Princess. That was Simon's business, not ours.

When he began to accompany us again, Bess said only, "I missed you."

"Your father needed me," he'd replied, smiling.

"That's different," she'd replied. "I must have a word with him tonight."

I made certain to warn Richard to be prepared.

WE WERE ROTATED back to England for two years, and given three weeks' leave when we arrived. Richard learned that Simon had nowhere to go and was planning to spend his leave in Hampshire at Regimental HQ.

After conferring with me, he offered Simon the cottage that stood on the other side of the wood that began at the bottom of our garden. It was just at the edge of our property, and the last occupant was the housekeeper for Richard's parents, who was offered it on her retirement. And she'd lived there until her death some years later. Simon was quite pleased, and before we were posted back to India, he asked Richard if he might buy the cottage and the land around it. The only stipulation that we put on the sale was that it would be sold back to us if ever Simon decided not to live there.

I had the strongest feeling that Richard was glad to have him close by. Bess certainly was, and I had to remind her that she mustn't make a nuisance of herself. There weren't many children her age close by, and so Simon often rode with her, played tennis with her, and generally tolerated her. But then he had no friends his own age, and he seldom went down to the pub for an evening. He had always been a great reader, and he mentioned once that he had an account at a bookshop in London.

We were sent back to India, and Richard was promoted to Colonel. That meant a great deal more responsibility, and he was often away or staying late into the evening on regimental business.

I watched Simon grow up. When he was promoted to Corporal, his duties increased and he too had less time for us, but off duty he was often to be found in the house or out with Bess. He never presumed on friendship or welcome—he always spoke to Richard first. And by now Bess had a new governess just out from England.

When the compound was attacked that awful day, and the main body of troops was out on Reconnaissance, we had a very difficult few hours. Bess, nine by then, had held up very well, better than her terrified governess. And help came in time. Simon slept in the house for quite a few nights after that, and other men took turns guarding the officers' quarters and the cantonment itself for almost a month, until all the men responsible had been found and sent under guard to Delhi.

I had expected Bess to be upset by all that had happened, but she was a soldier's daughter and told me when I'd asked if she had nightmares, "Not precisely nightmares, Mummy. Bad dreams, but I already know how it ended. So, they don't bother me all that much." Then she'd grinned. "Did you know that Miss now sleeps with a large revolver under her pillow?"

Shocked, I said, "Um, does she know how to use it?"

"I don't think so. And it isn't loaded. I've looked."

"I'm not sure I'm happy to hear there's a weapon in the Nursery."

"Don't worry, Mummy. I can load it if need be. But I'm not sure Miss can hit anything even if she tries to fire it."

I REMEMBER WHEN the turn of the century came that there was some discussion about whether 1900 was the end of the old century or the beginning of the next. And so, we had parties both years. As time passed, Simon was promoted to Corporal, then Sergeant, and finally became the youngest Sergeant Major in the history of the Regiment when the previous man retired. It was a popular choice, and he handled it well. Bess teased him unmercifully, but he just laughed.

And then May 1910, our lives changed dramatically.

In late March there was a raid on a friendly village at three o'clock in the morning. Richard, now a Colonel, went himself to deal with the aftermath, and when he came in at five o'clock, dusty and tired, he said, "I don't know who is behind the trouble. But I think we put the fear of God into them."

I'd reminded him that someone ought to tell the Pathans that.

And then toward the middle of May, the unthinkable happened, and none of us was prepared for it.

I sometimes have nightmares about it still. I've often wondered if Simon does as well . . .

THE RAID IN March was just the beginning of a period of unrest. Richard tracked the troublemakers to the Pass, caught them out in the open, and sent them racing for the Afghan border. After that, several companies kept a rotating watch on the mountainous Pass. Still, there had been two or three skirmishes, what Richard called a testing. To see where our strengths were, and of course our weaknesses, a constant probing. Several friendly villages were unsettled by the raiding parties, and they had to be both pacified and protected. We had heard there was civil unrest in other parts of the country as well, but whether this was in any way connected with our troubles, no one knew. Or if they did, no one was saying. Calcutta was being very quiet.

Afghanistan had been a thorn in Britain's side for a very long time. The country had attracted the attention of Russia as well as the British, and we had tried to influence the man on the throne—sometimes our puppet and sometimes not. Meanwhile the Afghans skillfully played both sides. In the first Afghan war, the retreating British columns were attacked repeatedly, enduring heavy casualties on their desperate march back to the Pass. That was in the 1830s and 40s. Another outbreak of hostilities took place in the late 1870s—just about the time Disraeli declared Victoria Empress of India—and in the end, Afghanistan was allowed to be independent. But we were not happy about that, as Russia kept up her own campaign to be the influencing partner there.

All this was in the past, of course, but was precisely why our cantonment had been set up and was still active all these years later. The Pass was the traditional gateway to India for invading armies. The Regiment was there to stop them.

The skirmishes became running battles, the probing more intense, and right in the middle of this, the Maharani's daughter—married and now a mother herself—decided to come and visit, bringing her youngest child with her while her husband and several of his Princely friends were busy entertaining dignitaries newly arrived in India.

It was the end of the dry season, when it was cooler and easier to travel any distance, and the heat would be climbing before the monsoon rains at the end of June. Still, the Maharani was excited, planning all manner of festivities, and I was at the Palace any number of times to help her decide such things as whether or not she ought to have her daughter's rooms redecorated, and what the guest list ought to be for various dinners.

Richard was asked to provide an escort, although the Princess would have retainers with her. It was more a matter of courtesy than need, but the train would include a great many trunks containing everything from nappies for the baby to the casket of jewels most of the Princes and their wives carried with them everywhere they went. And there would be bags of rupees as well, to pay for the journey and to give as baksheesh in princely style. Lieutenant Hayes was put in charge of the escort, and Simon was among the men he asked to accompany him.

Simon hadn't seen Parvati for some years, and I had no reason to speak to Richard about his being included in the escort. Nor did Simon ask to be relieved of duty.

The train brought the entourage most of the way, and then it had to caravan through the countryside to reach the Palace.

This much I knew—it's how replacements, friends like Melinda, visitors, and anyone else who comes out to us, must travel.

The rest I pieced together from a hodgepodge of truth and lies.

Disembarking from the train, Parvati spotted Simon among the escort. Not too difficult to do because he was often a head taller than the rest of the ranks. She greeted him as a friend, asked about us, and then proceeded through the station with the stationmaster escorting her, to the *shigram*, the bullock-drawn landau awaiting her outside. A nurse, rather broader than she was tall, easily carried the little girl, all big eyes and pretty silks. She was very like her mother, so it was said.

Parvati had already provided her husband with an heir, and marriage seemed to agree with her, for she was now a very attractive woman, with the poise and grace of her mother.

Eyes turned to follow her progress. And there was a delay while the many trunks were tied onto the carts that were to follow. The crowd of excited villagers who had come to stare at the spectacle had grown into about forty people.

Simon, seeing to the trunks, making certain they were lashed onto the wagons properly, had wisely posted a guard over them from luggage van to street.

While Lieutenant Hayes was chatting with the Princess, the Nanny was handed into the ornately decorated landau with the baby, toys and parasols and gold-tasseled cushions that alone cost more than most Indians made in a month. Some onlookers noticed that the child had a gold rattle in her fist, shaking it and cooing at the sound it made. The entourage slowly formed into a train of vehicles, trunks, staff, and Parvati at the head.

They set out, and in the heat of the day, they stopped to rest for an hour. They were to spend the night at a guesthouse halfway between the railhead and the Maharani's Palace. Advance parties had already inspected every inch of the guesthouse, and the apartments the Princess was to occupy had been emptied of their furnishings and all of them lavishly replaced with everything from a porcelain bath to silk hangings. One of the Palace cooks would be there to prepare her meals.

In late afternoon they had almost reached the guesthouse when Simon rode up beside the *shigram* and spoke to Parvati. They talked for several minutes, and then when the little girl began to cry irritably, Parvati looked for the gold rattle.

It was nowhere to be found, and the assumption was, it had fallen out of the carriage while the child was playing with it.

Simon volunteered to go back and look for it, although he had little hope of finding it. Something like the rattle would have meant a fortune to most of the people living out here.

Still, he found it in the dust kicked up by the bullock, a mile or so back, and as he caught up with the caravan, they were already disembarking and he saw to the unloading of the carts that one of the Princess's staff had indicated would be needed for the night. At this time the rattle was still in his possession.

He organized the horses, the parking of the wagons, and then when he finally reached the guesthouse, the Princess's party had already been taken up to the rooms reserved for them. Lieutenant Hayes saw Simon riding in and sent him to post a perimeter guard for the night, even though the compound was walled, with a gate.

At three in the morning, a guard making the rounds found a body beneath one of the carts, and signs that it had been tampered with. A chest lay on the ground, the lock broken and the contents missing.

There was a terrible uproar. Lieutenant Hayes was hard put to it to keep the Army escort and the Princess's entourage from each other's throats, each side pointing a finger at the other. He sent a mounted runner posthaste back to us, and I happened to be at home when the rider arrived, covered in dust and almost incoherent as he asked to speak to the Colonel.

Richard, unfortunately, was out with the troops, holding a series of talks with friendly elders on our side of the Pass. I took Private Evans across the compound to the Officer of the Day, where the man made his report.

Major Dudley was in charge, and he listened to what he was told, frowning and more than a little uncertain what to do about the situation.

There was no way to reach Richard. Nor was there time to do it. This was not something that could be left to Lieutenant Hayes to deal with, not with the political overtones, but I was very glad that Simon was there to support him.

"I'll have to go myself," the Major said finally. He thanked the runner, and then said to Captain Sullivan, "You'll take over here. I'll go out to that guesthouse, escort the Maharani's daughter directly to the Palace, and then do what I can to get to the bottom of what's happened." He shook his head. "This is damn—" Catching sight of me standing quietly to one side, he changed that to "—the worst possible timing."

I spoke then. "Major, it might be a good idea for me to ride with you. I know Parvati—the Princess—and I can soothe matters with the Maharani as well. A woman's touch?"

There was a brief flicker of relief in his face, and he said, "Thank you, Mrs. Crawford. Excellent idea." Turning to the men around him, he added, "See that a mount is ready for Mrs. Crawford. She will be joining the party. I think it best if we take other senior officers with us. Men who can be spared. We don't quite know what we'll be facing."

Captain Sullivan hurried away to make the arrangements, and the Major began to question the rider again, asking him who was in charge of the Princess's retinue.

I stayed just long enough to hear him say, "He's a right martinet, sir. Giving orders as if he outranked the Lieutenant. I'd walk wide of him, if I were you."

I was glad I'd spoken up. There was surely going to be trouble ahead, of one kind or another, and Richard would be glad of my account of events, when we got back.

It took me no time to change from my day dress to my riding habit, while my maid put the few things I'd need in a small case.

I was at the gate when Major Dudley rode up with the post adjutant, Captain Ramsey, and the senior regimental surgeon, Dr. Broughton.

Bess, just coming down the stairs, saw me leaving and ran out to ask where I was going. "I missed my ride this afternoon. Could I come with you?"

I told her only, "It seems that there's been a problem with the Princess's entourage. I'm going, in case there are any ruffled feathers that need smoothing. As I remember, the Prince is rather a stickler for propriety—"

"He's stuffy," Bess said. "I always felt sorry for Parvati, marrying him."

"He's young, darling. He'd only just inherited from his father a year before the wedding. He'll mellow as he gets the hang of being a Prince."

"I hope so for Parvati's sake. I liked her."

Giving her a last kiss, I mounted, and we set out.

None of us had much to say, until we were well clear of the cantonment. Then Major turned to me and asked quietly, "What can you tell me about this Princess? What am I to expect?"

"She's a little spoiled—the Maharani spoils all her children. But she was a lovely girl, and I've always liked her. Of course, it's been some years since I've seen her."

"Not much given to hysterics and crying, is she?"

I was already wishing Richard back here. "Not at all. At least not when she was sixteen."

"Just as well. We'll have trouble enough with the entourage. Who else is with Lieutenant Hayes? Besides the Sergeant Major? I didn't have time to review the roster."

"I don't know who else went with him. I didn't see them leave."

"Well. We must do what we can to see that the Princess is safe and no more disturbed than necessary. The rider doesn't know who the dead man is. That's a good sign. If he's just one of the people hired to bring the bullock carts, it should be a much simpler matter to deal with than one of the Prince's retainers."

I could have pointed out that while Lieutenant Hayes hadn't known more about the victim when he'd sent the mounted runner, he would surely know more now. He'd had two more hours to investigate. It would take us another two hours to reach the guesthouse—it was just after noon, now—and by that time, the whole affair might have blown over, the dead man's killer found and the Princess's party already on their way to the Maharani's Palace. Or by late afternoon, relations between the two parties, the men under Lieutenant Hayes and the Prince's retinue, might be on the point of armed warfare. We had no way of knowing. But I said nothing. I was here as a courtesy to the Princess, not to tell Major Dudley what to do.

But he turned to look at me, adding, "What's worrying me is jurisdiction here. Do we simply support whoever is in charge of the party, or do *we* take charge? And there's the location of the guesthouse. I'm not sure whose property that is. The Government's, surely?"

Major Dudley was a nice man, a good officer. But he was not a leader, and he had taken longer to reach his majority than Richard had done. He was a good party guest—he never brought up unpleasant subjects, he never gave anyone cause to object to anything he said or did. If we needed someone to dance with a widow or a young girl attending her first evening with her elders, he was willing, and he made his partner feel that he'd asked her for the pleasure of her company. He could hold down a fort, if he was called on to defend it, his tenacity coming to the fore. But he was not at his best where the situation was rapidly changing and evolving, and so it fell to the other officers to deal with incursions and raids, where split-second decisions made the difference between life and death. And he could be counted on to protect the cantonment.

I hoped that I could reassure Parvati that all was well, and that the Army had everything in hand, then whisk her off to her mother without further ado, while the authorities dealt with the murder and theft. It wouldn't interfere with her holiday at all.

The question was, had the man to whom the Prince had given the responsibility of protecting his wife and daughter also sent for instructions? The railway was not terribly far away, and there was a telegraph office. A single rider could be there and back in a quarter of the time a bullock cart could travel.

Apparently, we discovered when we arrived at the guesthouse, the Prince's man, one of his senior ministers, had indeed received instructions.

And was insisting that they be carried out to the letter.

Parvati and her little daughter had already been rushed off to the Palace under heavy escort, as if her life were in danger. The caravan had been hastily collected and was leaving shortly to follow her, accompanied by the rest of the troops and retinue, and there was already someone in custody, waiting to be taken away under a separate escort to stand trial. All very efficiently dealt with. Or so it appeared when we rode in finally and were greeted with this news by the beleaguered Sergeant at the gate.

Only, he was under strict orders from Lieutenant Hayes to

hold that gate and stop anyone from coming in or out, and he had armed men to back up those orders.

Not a very good sign that all was proceeding smoothly, I thought, when I saw how relieved the Sergeant was to see a senior officer arriving to take charge.

The gates swung open just wide enough to allow us through.

The courtyard was busy with the Prince's retainers, their brilliantly colored coats and signature turbans of the Prince's household moving about like birds of paradise among the plain clothing of the carters and the men who managed the bullocks. I'd learned to recognize most of the turban styles, especially those of the Salute Houses. The British had ranked the Princes by the number of guns in a salute a Prince received. As I recalled, this house had a 19-gun salute. Only three or four huge estates ranked 21 guns.

As we reached the front steps of the guesthouse, the Major and I found a very angry and red-faced Lieutenant Hayes, a very grim Sergeant Major, and a very stern Indian official informing them that, as this was a matter concerning the Prince's household, it was legally his right to take charge.

It *was* true that some of the more prominent Indian Princes had kept the right to deal with issues involving their estates or their families if their holdings were of a certain size. And Parvati's husband was most certainly one of them.

As we were approaching, Lieutenant Hayes looked up, saw us, and came forward to meet us. I watched the relief in his eyes fade as he realized that Colonel Crawford was not with us.

As we dismounted, he said in a low voice to the Major, "Thank God you're here. That man is one of the senior officials in the

Prince's household, and he's taking his prisoner back with him. And I've been trying to stall him for the past several hours. Come and talk some sense into him, sir!"

We hurried back with him, but the Prince's man and his escort were already turning to take his prisoner to horses stamping their feet in the shade of the only trees in the courtyard. Simon was still with them, and I saw him speaking to the Prince's man.

I thought he too was trying to reason with him, and then even as I watched, they met another of the Prince's men, coming toward them with chains in his hands. He lifted them and began to put them on Simon's wrists.

I had to bite off my shocked exclamation. "Oh—"

Major Dudley was already following them, and I made certain that I was behind the Major with the Lieutenant and the others as they caught up with the escort.

"What is this?" the Major snapped. "I am the senior officer here. Explain to me what you are doing with this man?"

The Prince's man turned, his eyebrows raised. He was not as tall as the Major or Simon, but had an air about him that told me he wasn't accustomed to being questioned. He said, "This man is guilty of the murder of one of the Prince's servants and the theft of items belonging to the Prince. We are returning with him to the Prince's court."

"I was told it was the owner of a bullock cart who was killed."

"Nevertheless. He was hired by the Household. And as such we are responsible for him, not the Army."

Simon had turned, his mouth in a tight line, his gaze finding and meeting mine. I tried to give him a reassuring smile.

"*This* man?" the Major was saying. "He's a soldier of the King of England. You'll do nothing of the sort. If there has been a crime committed, his commanding officer will sort it out and bring the appropriate charges."

I saw the bruise on Simon's cheekbone, then. He'd given someone an excuse to strike him.

"There are no 'appropriate charges.' This is a matter of murder." The Prince's minister turned slightly to point. A wagon was standing just beyond the horses. "The dead man is being returned to his family for burial. The evidence is locked in a strongbox to be presented to the Prince."

"I have no objection to the dead man being returned to his family. But not until I have had an Army surgeon and witnesses view the body."

There was heated discussion about this.

In the end, the Prince's man—I still hadn't caught his name—relented, and the entire party made their way past the horses and over to the wagon.

There were flies everywhere. Brushing them aside, we reached the wagon, and Dr. Broughton stopped me from approaching. "This isn't something you should have to view, Mrs. Crawford."

Reluctantly I stepped aside. But I knew Richard was going to want to know even the tiniest detail. And while I had my back to the wagon, I was still close enough to hear what was being said.

It was enclosed, that wagon, but in the heat of India, bodies don't fare very well, and I heard the discussion about how to unwrap the dead man so that he could be covered again as neatly as before.

That went on for several minutes.

Simon's guards were watching events as well, and I moved slightly so that I was nearer him. Bess had told me once that he'd helped her with her French, and so I said, in my own schoolgirl French, "What's happening?"

"They refuse to listen."

"Is Parvati all right?"

"I believe so."

The Prince's man turned and said, "There will be no conversation with the prisoner, if you please."

The adjutant, Captain Ramsey, said, "On the contrary, I will hear his account of events before he goes anywhere."

There was more discussion, and the Prince's man was growing quite angry by this time.

Finally they agreed on unwrapping the body, and the process began.

After several minutes, I heard the surgeon say, "There appear to be two wounds, very close together. Knife, like a bayonet thrust, up to the heart. He would have died instantly."

That was precisely how an Army surgeon would describe a wound, I thought, but why on earth had he used the term *bayonet* just now? When a trained soldier was accused of the crime?

"Precisely," the Prince's man was saying, echoing my own thought, "A soldier's thrust."

They argued over that for several minutes more. Simon, saying nothing, was standing there bareheaded in the heat, as stoic as I'd ever seen him.

Finally, the Prince's man ordered the victim to be covered again.

Major Dudley said flatly, "We will adjourn to a room in the guesthouse. Lieutenant, what facilities do they have?"

"There's a large room on the first floor where meals are served."

He turned to one of his men and ordered him to go and commandeer the room.

"We are leaving," the Prince's man said adamantly.

"Not until we've learned what the evidence is here. You would not allow one of your own men to be taken away until you had been told why. With that in mind, we will go inside where there is a certain amount of privacy to be had."

The Prince's man was not having it.

Major Dudley said shortly, "You are not on your master's estate at this moment, sir, and you would do well to remember that."

In the end, he capitulated, and the entire party moved back across the courtyard to the guesthouse doors.

I was surprised to find that the Major was right. We'd collected quite a crowd of onlookers, and I made a point to scan the faces nearest us, then those farther back. But there was only simple curiosity here. No one appeared to look guilty or anxious.

Of course, it couldn't have ended that simply, the murderer betraying himself just when we needed it. With a sigh, I made a point to follow the others.

The Prince's man said, "The lady need not accompany us."

To my surprise, it was Major Dudley who said, "She is present as a friend of the Maharani's. She will hear what we hear."

The Prince's man looked me over, then nodded. But he wasn't pleased about this either. Had he already sent messages to the Maharani? Surely Parvati could have spoken up for Simon! But then she hadn't seen him since she was sixteen . . .

We went inside the guesthouse, climbed a dark staircase, and found the room that Lieutenant Hayes had spoken of.

It was darkly paneled too, reminding me of the room at the

Four Doves in our village in Somerset, sometimes used for inquests. Only there wasn't a coroner, a police officer to give testimony, or any of the other usual parties one expected to see here in this dark little chamber. The overhead lamps, more Indian than English, cast shadows on our faces as someone moved to turn them up.

There was uncertainty about where everyone was to sit. As the men worked that out, I stayed near the door. Simon waited quietly, his back against the wall nearest the door. The chains on his wrists look heavy, but he didn't pay any attention to them.

I thought, *This must be the face that Richard saw on raids. Quiet, competent, ready to follow orders.*

But he must have been aware of the danger in which he stood. What was he thinking? I wished I knew.

The Major and the Prince's man finally sat down at opposite ends of the long table at one end of the room, and after some uncertainty the others who had come with us chose chairs that roughly aligned them on the two sides. I noticed that Corporal Stevens, one of the men who had come with the original party under Lieutenant Hayes, stayed close by Simon, as if ready to cover his escape. He was standing there by the wall, one of the Prince's men on either side of him. He was taller than either of them.

Just then one of the entourage came hurrying in, bowed to the Prince's man, then whispered in his ear. He listened, shook his head, and waved the man away.

The Major cleared his throat, then turned to Lieutenant Hayes. "Very well, Lieutenant, take us through your activities from the time the royal train arrived at the station."

Lieutenant Hayes, after a hasty glance in Simon's direction, began his report, indicating how he'd set his men to guard the arrivals, and how the bullock carts had been ordered in the long line that made up the caravan. He carried on through the brief stop along the way, to rest the animals, and then the arrival here.

It was a straightforward account. I'd heard men coming into the house late in the evening, for various reasons unable to leave their reports until morning. I knew that Lieutenant Hayes was being as accurate as he could be, neither leaving out anything nor putting anything in for Simon's sake.

But he was one man. He couldn't be everywhere, and there were gaps in his testimony because of that.

The Major asked, "The man who was killed. Did you see him during the morning? Or on the road here?"

"No, sir. I mean to say, I was aware of the men and women in the Princess's entourage, and I was aware of the men who dealt with the carts. I couldn't tell you which of the carts that man drove. Given the size of the party, I was working with numbers rather than faces."

"Did you know he belonged to the caravan, when his body was found?"

"Yes, sir. He wasn't wearing the Prince's livery. That meant he had been hired to meet the party at the railway station. One of the other bullock cart owners told us who he was and why he was here. I accepted that as sufficient identification. And the guest-house gates had been locked at sunset—no one could come in or go out without an alarm being raised."

"Who found the body?"

"Private Henley, sir. He was walking down the line of carts, having taken over from Private Johnston. The night had been quiet—he hadn't expected trouble. Then he saw a man's bare heel sticking out from under the side of the cart, and went over to investigate. The man didn't respond when Private Henley touched his foot, and he reached down to pull the man out into the open. He lit a match, realized the man had been stabbed, and saw too that someone had cut the corner ropes holding down the canvas covering, apparently intending to steal something from the cart. As Private Henley cast about, he noticed a small casket lying just behind the wheel, upside down and empty. No weapon was visible, although Private Henley had the presence of mind to look under that wagon and those on either side, after he'd shouted the alarm. Later, when one of the entourage was brought over to tell us what was missing, he informed us that the casket had contained rupees. Silver, Edward VII on the face. And a gold chain, heavy, about thirty inches long."

"Carry on."

For the first time Lieutenant Hayes took a deep breath, as if bracing himself.

"First I ran a head count, to see if anyone had gone missing. But everyone was present and accounted for, except the cart owner, of course. And everyone except the men on guard claimed to have been asleep. Still, I made an effort to ascertain the whereabouts of everyone in the party. I asked Sergeant Major Brandon to assist because of the number of people involved. As the officer in charge I took it upon myself to deal with the people closest to the Princess, while Sergeant Major Brandon dealt with the carters. Next I ordered everyone searched, except the Princess and her women. I paired one of my men with one of the Prince's staff, and they went through everything, including the carriages and the carts, even the harnesses for the oxen and their bags of feed."

"And then?" the Major prompted, when the Lieutenant hesitated a second time.

The Lieutenant looked across the room toward where Simon was standing, then his gaze moved on to me before he answered the question.

"When the search was finished, I myself searched the belongings of the two men who carried out the main search."

There was a long pause. Then Lieutenant Hayes added, "The Prince's man was clean. In Sergeant Major Brandon's saddlebags I found a gold rattle that I was told belonged to the little girl. And a handful of silver rupees identical to those I was told were in the casket. I didn't find the gold chain."

It was all I could do not to gasp.

Major Dudley made an effort not to look in Simon's direction. After a moment he said, "And the murder weapon? The knife?"

"We haven't found it. Nor the rest of the rupees nor the gold chain."

"What did Brandon have to say for himself?"

"The rupees are his, nothing to do with those that were stolen. The rattle was lost by the little girl earlier in the day. He found it and hadn't reached the guesthouse until the ladies had already gone to their quarters. None of her women were about, and he put the rattle in his saddlebags until he could return it."

"Does Sergeant Major Brandon have any knives in his possession?"

"Yes, sir. One."

"Could it have made the wounds in the dead man's body?"

"It's possible, sir. I can't say for certain. We examined his knife very carefully. If it was used, he'd cleaned it well afterward."

I had been watching Simon's face. It was impassive. But the

Prince's man was triumphant. He could already feel himself vindicated in taking Simon back to be tried.

None of this fit the young man I knew, who came and went in our house, whom we trusted with our daughter. The rattle aside, I couldn't picture him robbing a cart, much less stabbing the owner.

And all my instincts urged me to *do* something. Before it was too late.

Major Dudley finally turned to Simon.

"Have you anything to say on your own behalf, Sergeant Major?"

"Only that I've told you the truth."

"It will show good faith, if you tell us where the other items have been hidden."

"I can't tell you what I don't know, sir."

I was wishing with all my heart that Richard was here. To speak up, to do something. I was wishing that the door to this stuffy little room would suddenly be flung open and that he'd march in and demand to be heard.

He hadn't been here when the crime had been done. For that matter, neither had I. But Richard would fight for Simon, and in his place, I must do the same.

It was up to me. The only woman in a room full of angry men.

I stepped forward. "May I ask a question, Major Dudley? On behalf of the Maharani." I'd been around the Army for years. Rank didn't put me off.

"Please do, Mrs. Crawford." He seemed to be grateful for the interruption.

"Sergeant Major Brandon has told you how he came by the rattle. Have you asked the Princess whether his account is true or not? If the rattle belongs to the child, she may know if it was lost or misplaced. Or stolen."

The Prince's man interrupted. "She will not be disturbed by this matter."

"The rattle is hers, sir," I countered. "She must be asked what she believes became of it. If she agrees that the Sergeant Major's account is true, then he cannot be charged with having that in his possession."

"This is a child's toy, Mrs. Crawford. It is not likely to be in the possession of a British soldier. If the prisoner had found it, as he claimed, he would have given it to someone on the staff to take to the child. He saw the rattle, and it tempted him to search for more. Who better to know which cart contained the Princess's jewels? He had been responsible for their protection."

A thought occurred to me. Simon had once thought that he was in love with Parvati. Had he held on to the rattle as an excuse to speak to her again in the morning—this morning—before they set out?

But I couldn't put that question to him. It would seal his fate in the eyes of the Prince's man.

Instead, I asked, "I should like to know why the Sergeant Major—who has known the Princess's family for a number of years—would wish to rob her." I turned to Simon. "Do you owe anyone money? Do you have gambling debts?"

"No, ma'am. Nor do I gamble, more than an occasional barracks game for small sums."

"Was there a reason other than personal gain why you should have taken anything from the Prince's family? Any enmity toward them?"

"No, ma'am. I don't believe I have ever met the Prince."

"You have met the Maharani. You have seen her children come and go in the Palace. They play with my daughter. Is there any reason for you to harm her family?"

"No, ma'am." His voice was calm, steady. He had learned that supporting Richard when there was trouble along the Pass. It occurred to me that he expected to be treated fairly here in this room. And because of that, he had no reason to be afraid.

"How many times have you spoken to the Princess during this journey?"

"Twice. At the station and later when the baby was irritable from the heat and the dust. I rode up beside the landau, hoping to distract her. That was when the Princess couldn't find the rattle and was afraid it had been lost."

"Why did you think you might distract the little girl?"

There was the trace of a smile. "Experience with your daughter at the age of five, ma'am."

"And you saw this as an opportunity to ride back along the road in the hope of finding it, because it was valuable and you wanted to keep it?"

"I came to the guesthouse, intending to return it, but the entourage had retired to their quarters, and I was ordered to set the guard instead of waiting until someone came down again. It was late when I returned, and the party had already finished their supper and retired. There was no one I could trust to see that the rattle was taken up to the Princess or the nursemaid."

I looked at the Major. "Is this true?"

"I can vouch for the fact that Sergeant Major Brandon came to the door as I was leaving, and I gave him his orders. None of us stayed in the guesthouse. The rooms had been given over to the Princess and her entourage. We were to bivouac on the grounds."

"Then I suggest that we continue our journey, and when we have reached the Palace, I will ask the Maharani if I may speak to her daughter, to see if she confirms or denies the Sergeant Major's account."

"I agree," Major Dudley put in quickly. "With those additional facts in hand, in my opinion the Sergeant Major must be tried by a court martial, where all this information can be properly examined."

The Prince's man stood then. "This is not a military matter. It is a simple case of theft and murder. That remains, whether the matter of the rattle is settled or not. And Her Highness cannot speak to what happened in the lines, where a man was killed. My master will be expecting me to bring this soldier back with me, to await trial as soon as the Prince returns."

"Then the question must be, did this man, this cart owner, have enemies? Is that why he is dead?" I asked. "Does anyone know anything about his past?"

"He was guarding the property of His Highness. And he was killed because he tried to prevent the looting of the Prince's property by this soldier."

I turned to Major Dudley, expecting him to stand by Simon.

Instead he replied, "He has a point. This death occurred because of theft of the property belonging to the Princess. And the dead man is not an ordinary civilian, he was a member of the Prince's party, if only for the journey to the Maharani's Palace. I find it difficult to know just how we have the right to change the rules. It's the Princess who has been wronged, not the Army. Although I'm reluctant to agree, I can't see a clear reason to prevent the Sergeant Major being taken away and tried in the Prince's state. With the stipulation of course of the Army overseeing proceedings. And if the Princess can't be made available, the child's nursemaid being sent for."

The doctor spoke then. "I disagree. The weapon used to kill the victim hasn't been found. There are no traces of blood on the knife belonging to the Sergeant Major. And no bloody cloths or clothes discovered in his belongings. And there would have been a great deal of blood. There are no witnesses to the Sergeant Major having been seen in the lines at the time of this murder. Except for the discovery of the child's rattle, there is nothing here to link one of Her Majesty's soldiers to this murder."

The Captain spoke then. "There is the further matter of jurisdiction. This is neither the Prince's lands nor an Army cantonment. Therefore, I recommend that we send this matter to Calcutta. Lord Minto's writ extends to all of India that is not a part of a Princely estate. That would apply in this instance."

The arguments went on for another hour. Once Major Dudley had made his view known, the Prince's man wouldn't hear of any other point of view.

Finally, the man stood up and said, "To disagree further is to cast doubt on the integrity of the Prince's court. His Highness will not be happy to hear this."

I had no idea whether the Prince's courts were fair or not. This man was determined to keep Simon in his grip and not let him go. That made me wonder if the Prince was such an upstanding man after all, because his representative here seemed to be in no mood to cross him.

I said, "I cannot see how taking the matter to Calcutta is any reflection on the Prince's justice. If the Governor-General feels that he has no jurisdiction, then he will send this matter where it belongs."

"The law is clear on this matter," the Prince's man told me bluntly. "There is no need to trouble Calcutta at this time."

I was beginning to think he disliked me—the look he gave me would surely have stopped a locomotive in its tracks. Well, I didn't care very much for him either.

I wanted to shout him down, but I knew that would be disastrous. The only way to help Simon was to keep my head and think clearly.

"Perhaps that's the very reason we should take this trial to Calcutta. You have given us no evidence to speak of. How many people were in this caravan yesterday? What have they told you about the dead man? Or who among them might be a thief, tempted by what those carts were carrying? And you have not found the golden chain. Where is that? Or the rest of the rupees?" I asked. "The Maharani will wish to know these things."

"We questioned the owners of the carts. They could only tell us that the dead man was new to the district. And not one of them has a record for thieving." There was scorn in his voice. Then he turned to the Major.

"We have listened with courtesy. Now we must ask you to step aside and allow us to take the prisoner in charge."

I could see that the Major was wavering, despite the disapproval of Dr. Broughton and Captain Ramsey. And so, I made the best of a bad bargain. I said, "Very well. If the Sergeant Major is taken out of the Army's hands, officers from his Regiment must accompany him, to be certain that he receives a fair trial. With all respect due to the Prince, His Majesty the King Emperor would not wish it to be otherwise. He had always had a strong affection for the Army. And I believe when it comes down to it, his wishes are paramount."

"We cannot know what His Majesty's wishes might be in this matter. He is dead." His voice was cold.

There was absolute shock in the room, a silence that went on for a stretch of seconds. King Edward had only been on the throne for—I quickly counted—nine years but he was very popular. I tried to take it in, and it was impossible.

And then the thought came. *Dear God—not now!*

The Prince's man waited a moment, clearly relishing the effect his words had had. Then he added, "The shoot has been canceled, and the dignitaries have returned to Calcutta. The Prince is already on his way back to Rulumpur."

That broke the spell.

The table was suddenly in an uproar.

Major Dudley's voice exclaimed, forceful enough to be heard over everyone else. *"You cannot know that—"*

"A runner has just reported this to me. You saw him yourself. King Edward died at Buckingham Palace on the tenth of this month."

There was no way to prove or disprove this news.

And every one of us there, shaken as we were, knew that the Governor-General and everyone else in Calcutta would have no time for anything else, just now.

There were more questions. In the disarray at the table, watched by nearly everyone in the room, I managed to catch Simon's eye. I smiled, silently formed a single word. *"Richard."*

In the end I got my way. The doctor, the adjutant, and Lieutenant Hayes went with the party carrying Simon to Lahore and from there to the Prince's home, to await the arrival of the Prince himself.

I asked to go as well, but I was told it would not be proper, as I was a woman and there were no facilities for me as we traveled.

I asked permission to speak to Simon privately before their departure, but that too was denied.

My last sight of him was as he was led out the door. Leg irons had been added to the chains around his wrists. I felt like weeping. I'd tried so very hard, and it still wasn't enough.

But there was no time for weakness.

While the Prince's man was making final the arrangements for splitting the caravan, some to return with the prisoner, others to continue on their way, I took Lieutenant Hayes aside.

"I need to see where the murder happened," I told him urgently.

"I don't know—" he began, still flustered by the turn of events.

"The Maharani will wish to know what I saw. And the Colonel as well."

"I—yes, of course—this way."

The wagons had been drawn up in the rear the courtyard, ranked by what they carried. The less important their load, the farther toward the back wall of the compound.

I didn't know the Lieutenant well. He was of medium height, fair hair and skin that turned red in the sun's heat. His eyes were a blue-gray. And he'd just returned from leave in England, this time bringing his wife back with him. She had always stayed behind, reluctant to leave her parents, but he had persuaded her to join him, and whenever I'd spoken to her, she'd seemed more than a little overwhelmed.

We found the proper wagon, still in its place but under heavy guard, now that everyone knew what it carried. It was to continue to the Maharani's Palace with the Regiment's escort and some of the Prince's people to ensure it arrived safely. I could see the black stain in the earth by one wheel. Blood, I realized, still drawing flies. That was where the man had been killed.

Just above the spot, I could see that someone had taken a knife to the heavy ropes that held down the canvas that covered the cart. Just above that, a slice in the fabric itself had been hurriedly patched.

We walked around it, then I knelt in the dust to look under it. But there was no sign of a knife. Had the killer taken it with him?

I turned. The high wall around the guesthouse was some thirty feet away. Still, it was close enough for someone to run toward it and throw a heavy knife over the top of it.

I said to the Lieutenant, "Has anyone searched the outside of that wall?"

"Er—no, ma'am. I don't believe that was done."

"Find two of our men and have them walk the perimeter with you. I'll stand here, so you will know where to look. But keep a sharp eye out for anything that might help."

He wasn't used to taking orders from one of the Regiment's wives. But he was a good man, and after the briefest hesitation, he nodded. "He could have just that, hoping to collect it later. God knows, there must be a hundred knives amongst the Prince's men. Ceremonial and real. We looked at each one."

"I don't think he expected to be disturbed. He might have panicked, got rid of the knife. It's worthwhile checking."

And he was gone. I walked toward the wall, standing just a

few feet from it. Vines covered part of it, but they weren't thick enough to hold a knife, even if it had landed short and fallen in them.

I heard a shout, and the Lieutenant called, "Mrs. Crawford? Are you there?"

"Keep moving toward the sound of my voice. I think you may be about fifteen feet short."

There was a tap on the wall. "Yes, that's right," I said.

I could hear men talking, but not what they were talking about. After several minutes they moved on.

I left the wall, then, and hurried toward the gates in front of the guesthouse.

I hadn't been there very long when the Lieutenant, Private Jeffers, and Private Dunn walked through. I couldn't tell from their expressions whether they'd found anything or not.

The Lieutenant gestured for me to follow him, and out of sight of the Prince's camp, we stepped inside one of the Army tents that hadn't yet been taken down. "Look at this," he said quietly, and opening his tunic he took out a rather dirty silk handkerchief and set it down on a camp table. I saw then that the stiff, dark stains weren't earth, they were blood. With the two Privates as our witnesses, he unrolled the handkerchief to reveal a long, narrow-bladed knife, a gold chain, and a sack of silver rupees. "I didn't see it, actually," he was explaining quietly. "I stumbled over some half-hidden stones, and when I looked down, I realized the earth around them was loose. A little digging brought this to light. It had been hastily, but carefully buried."

"The gates were closed when we arrived. When could someone have buried these?" I asked, curious.

"That's just it, they were opened while the Princess's entourage was being collected. Anyone could have slipped out then—there was a lot of confusion. What should I do with this?" He cleared his throat. "Major Dudley *could* tell me to hand it over to the Prince's man, now. But I don't trust him, Mrs. Crawford. He could easily swear later that he never had it in his possession."

The knife was similar to those I'd seen in the bazaar shops, popular and cheap, although the steel was good. Villagers kept them sharp and used them for any number of things. When I touched the blade with my fingertip, it came away a rusty red, and I hastily wiped my fingers on my own handkerchief. The rupees were Edward VII, common enough. The chain however was heavy gold, distinctive. Broken up and sold, it could keep a poor family in food for a year.

"Give it to me," I said finally. "This should go to the Maharani. Her word against that of the Prince's man will carry more weight than ours. But I'm swearing all three of you to secrecy, do you understand? No gossip about this in the barracks." But I knew already that for Simon's sake, they wouldn't talk. "I will tell the Colonel, no one else. Not even the Sergeant Major, if they let me have a final word with him. You may be called as witnesses later. Are you prepared to testify?"

Both men agreed that they were—they were even eager to go with the officers following Simon. But Lieutenant Hayes had reservations.

"Are you sure, ma'am, that this is the way to handle it?" he asked, worry in his voice. "Begging your pardon, but I'd as soon throw this in that man's face straightaway. Very publicly."

"If *we* give it to the Prince, he will say that we knew where Simon had hidden it, and are trying to do this now to clear him of blame. It's safer with the Maharani." Even as I said that, I could only hope that it was true.

"But Sergeant Major Brandon doesn't have silk handkerchiefs, ma'am," Private Dunn said. "We have cotton or linen."

"Handkerchiefs can be stolen. Unfortunately, there doesn't appear to be any identifying marks on it." I looked at it carefully. "No initials. Not even the Prince's coat of arms. Nor is it something one of the carters might own." And that brought me back to my earlier thought, that it was possible the Prince's minister was busy protecting his master's good name. Better a soldier to take the blame . . .

Lieutenant Hayes gestured to the two privates standing there watching us. "Take them home with you, ma'am. Where the Maharani can have them questioned. Don't let them go anywhere else."

"Yes, that's probably for the best. Let them escort me."

"Begging your pardon, ma'am, but I wish the Colonel was here in your place!"

"I do as well, Lieutenant," I responded fervently.

The chaos in the courtyard had sorted itself out, and the caravan, much shorter already, had finally been divided to the Prince's man's liking. I kept watching for any sign of Simon, but the Prince's men were keeping him incommunicado.

It occurred to me then that perhaps they were afraid for him to speak to *us*, not the other way around.

But *why*?

I hadn't had a great deal of contact with members of the Princely Houses. I'd met quite a few of them at durbars for notable guests, but not to speak to for any length of time. I was after all the wife of a serving officer, and not particularly important myself. But they had been gracious and I'd liked most of them. More to the point, they had liked Richard, talking to him at length about the Frontier and interested in his point of view. But sometimes retainers are haughtier than their masters . . .

I found myself thinking that we should have brought the chaplain with us, in place of the doctor.

And as I formed that thought, a brilliant idea seemed to burst into my head, giving me sudden hope.

I went to find the doctor, who was conferring with Captain Ramsey, the adjutant, in a quiet corner of the chaos.

He turned at once to me, saying, "This is a grave situation, Mrs. Crawford. I needn't tell you that."

Apparently he and the Major were quite concerned about abandoning me, as it were, as they'd tried to provide for my return to the cantonment.

"I don't know how else to arrange the officers," the Captain was saying. "You should have a larger escort. It isn't safe for you to be riding that far alone. Would you consider going first to the Maharani's?"

"I appreciate your concern, gentlemen. But someone has to be there when the Colonel Sahib rides in sometime tonight or tomorrow, to see that he hears a straight account of this business. I'm perfectly capable of doing that. The Major must accompany the caravan to the Maharani's to be sure it arrives safely, and *she* is given a full account. Her daughter left before the charges were brought against the Sergeant Major, but she may know something helpful. And you must go with the Sergeant Major to see that he's treated fairly. Richard will follow as quickly as he can."

The doctor said, "We're leaving the cantonment very short-handed as it is. For all we know, this theft and murder were staged, to allow the Regiment to be stripped, officers heading out in every direction. I wouldn't put it past some of those tribes to consider such a game. And if there's an attack coming, we'll be hard-pressed to deal with it."

Lieutenant Hayes, who heard that as he joined us, seemed to be less worried. "I can't see the Prince's people conspiring with the Frontier tribes."

"There needn't be a conspiracy. One man—a bullock driver, even someone following the retinue at a distance, waiting his chance—could be here to start trouble," Captain Ramsey agreed.

I replied, "It's Sergeant Major Brandon who is in danger at the moment." Then, looking around the four of us, to be sure we couldn't be overheard, I added, "I need your help, Doctor. Do you mind lying in a good cause?"

He smiled. "It depends on the cause."

And I explained. "Could you demand to see the Sergeant Major, because he has a health condition that you wish to be certain will not cause trouble during the journey to Rulumpur?"

"What sort of health issues, Mrs. Crawford?"

"Any that you might come up with. They're refusing to let us speak to him. And in examining him, you might be able to find out more about what happened than we know now."

He considered the question. "I'm willing to try." With a nod to me, he set out across the compound, and I saw him engage in a heated discussion with the men guarding the prisoner. A few minutes later, he went to find the Prince's man. And ten minutes later, rather red in the face, Dr. Broughton went back to where

Simon was waiting and told his guards in no uncertain terms that he was going to speak to their prisoner.

At a sign from the Prince's man, standing by the steps of the guesthouse, the guards let Dr. Broughton pass, and he began to look at Simon's eyes, examining his neck and shoulders—and managed to swing him around where neither the guards nor the Prince's man could watch the prisoner's face. The doctor, head bent to listen to Simon's heart, finally looked up, then nodded toward the Prince.

"He'll do," he called, and stalked off. He didn't come directly back to where we were waiting, instead speaking to a private soldier and then a Sergeant, as if asking about their healing wounds, for the Sergeant rolled up his sleeve and presented his forearm for the doctor to examine closely. Then the private pulled up his trouser leg and presented his calf.

By the time he had come back to where we were standing, I thought he must have examined half the entire British Army.

There was a successful gleam in his eye as he escorted me to where my mount was waiting, and as he gave me a lift up into the saddle, he said quietly, "Something to do with the Princess. Brandon understands their language, and he overheard the Prince's man speaking to one of the entourage. There was concern for her safety."

My heart sank. Clearly there was more to what was happening than some conspiracy by the Frontier tribes. They had rushed Parvati away, but with all these soldiers and her personal retinue, not even counting the Prince's household escorting her, she was as safe here as she was in the zenana, the women's quarters at Rulumpur.

"I'm sorry," the doctor said. "But I shall use that excuse to speak to the prisoner again, you may be sure. If you're asked, it was a war wound—there's a bit of metal lodged near his heart. It might keep them from knocking him about, when they have the chance."

I smiled, although I didn't feel much like it. "Thank you, Doctor. If I had my way, I'd see you mentioned in dispatches."

He laughed, gave me a half salute, and walked back to where the adjutant and the Lieutenant were preparing to ride out. While we'd been talking, the doctor and I, Simon had been put in one of the wagons. I turned my horse toward the gate, where the road began, hoping for a last glimpse of him.

And then he was gone, the bullocks moving slowly out into the dust of the road, and his wagon jerking and bouncing behind the team as it turned back toward the railway station.

And even though I tried to see Simon inside that closed carriage, I couldn't. But I hoped to heaven he could see me.

My escorts and I were the very last to leave the compound. I'd made certain that Major Dudley had gone with the carts destined for the Maharani's Palace, and that the other three officers had indeed been allowed to accompany Simon. And only then did I begin the long ride back to the cantonment.

Ever since I had ridden into the guesthouse compound, I'd concentrated on what was happening to Simon. I'd fought to keep my wits about me. I'd put my concern for him ahead of my own growing sense of helplessness as it became clear that we couldn't budge the Prince's man.

And now the letdown followed. I needed a good cry, I realized, a woman's way of letting the increasing pressures of the day dissipate even as the fear was building inside me that we could very well lose Simon. But the two men with me would be shocked to see the Colonel's lady in tears. And so, I held them back.

I ARRIVED BACK at the cantonment safe and sound—and very tired, more from worry than from the distance—long before Richard rode in with the rest of the troops.

Bess had held supper for me—I realized all at once that I'd missed my dinner entirely, and hadn't even noticed—and her first words were, "You look so tired. This wasn't just a ride, was it? What's happened?"

She was so perceptive, my daughter.

"Trouble with the Princess's party. But it's sorted, now. She should be at the Palace, settling in for her visit."

She frowned. "I didn't hear the escort riding in with you."

"No, I came on ahead. They'll be home tomorrow if not this evening. I didn't care to spoil the Maharani's happiness by hanging about. We can visit later." I wasn't precisely lying to her, but I knew my daughter. If she learned why Simon hadn't come back with us, she would go directly to the Maharani, and demand that he be set free. And much as I wished that would be enough to free him, I was beginning to think that this affair was far more complicated than I'd realized, even there in that stuffy room in the guesthouse when it had seemed bad enough. "Let me freshen up, and I'll come down for supper."

Escaping to my room, I stood for a moment in the middle of the floor, staring at that image of Simon in chains. I couldn't get it out of my mind. He wasn't my child, but he'd been like a son to us, and I had fought for him, just as if he had been our flesh and blood. But I didn't cry, there in my room. I refused to cry. That was admitting defeat, even before I'd spoken to Richard.

The maid came with hot water and fresh towels, and I took the time to wash my face and clean off the dust and heat of travel. Then I changed into my evening clothes, just as if we were all sitting down to dinner.

I don't remember what we ate, Bess and I. And afterward we took our tea in my sitting room. I must have put up a good enough front, for Bess kissed me good night and went up to bed at the usual hour.

When I was sure she was settled, I sat there, a shawl around my shoulders against the cool of the evening at this time of year. Waiting. Trying not to remember . . .

It was well after four in the morning when at last I heard the horses coming in, and half an hour later, Richard came quietly through the door.

When he saw me sitting there in the dark, he said at once, "What's wrong?"

I was glad my escort had kept their promise not to say anything to anyone. I hadn't wanted such news spreading through the barracks before Richard had heard it.

"Darling, come walk with me in the garden. I don't want us to be overheard."

And so we went out to the gardens, and there I told him all that I knew about what had happened at the guesthouse.

He didn't say a word until I'd finished, but I was standing close to him and could feel the rising tension in him as he listened.

"Major Dudley hasn't come back from the Palace, yet. Or at least he hasn't stopped here. So, I can't tell you how the Maharani has taken all this. I don't know what Parvati herself knows. I can't think why Simon believes this somehow has to do with her. But if he says it does, then that's where we must start. I intend to call on the Maharani tomorrow as early as I can."

Richard took a deep breath. "Damn!" he said softly. But in the quiet darkness, I heard him.

"I don't know what else we can do," I said. "But we must think of something. Simon isn't guilty of this. And I don't trust that man of the Prince's."

"Do you believe that someone planned this? To trap Simon?"

I hadn't shown Richard the items in my possession—the handkerchief, the knife, and the things supposedly taken from the small box. But I'd explained what the Lieutenant had found on the far side of the wall.

When I didn't answer straightaway, Richard went on. "I can understand someone thinking that here was a cart full of treasures—clothes with jewels sewn into them, headdresses heavy with gold, hangings of the best silks for the Princess's rooms. God knows what else. And a poor man might decide that one small casket wouldn't be missed until much later. In that case, why didn't he take the contents with him? Why leave them where they might be found, after having to do murder to keep them at the start?"

"The gates were locked and guarded," I reminded him. "He might have tossed the knife and the other things over the wall, expecting to collect them afterward. But that doesn't explain them being buried, does it? If he had time to bury them, why not simply take them away with him as soon as he collected them?"

"Because everyone would be searched. And his absence would have been noticed. The hunt would begin."

"We must be there at the trial, Richard. I won't sit here and wait for news."

He pulled me into his arms, comforting me. "No. I think we were successful enough last night to keep the Frontier pacified for the moment. Tomorrow, you must call on the Maharani and tell her what you know. All of it."

I sighed. "I felt so very helpless as I watched Simon standing there, chains on his wrists, and I couldn't stop them from taking him away."

"You made them allow officers to accompany the party. Simon isn't alone."

"Still—*why*? It makes no sense that one of the Princely Houses would choose to alienate the Army like this."

"God knows. But I will find out."

I knew that tone of voice. Richard would indeed get to the bottom of this.

I remembered as we were walking back to the house. "Is it true that the King is dead?" I had never had a chance to take that in, much less think about it until now.

"I don't know. This is the first I've heard of it. Calcutta will be sending out word, I'm sure." He frowned. "In the last newspapers we got, I'm sure it said he was in Biarritz. Queen Mary was in Greece visiting her brother. Surely if the King *was* ill, she'd have been with him."

I WENT TO call on the Maharani just after eleven the next morning. Bess had asked to come with me, but I told her that this was more or less an official visit, as the Colonel's wife, and we'd call again tomorrow. She was disappointed, but she understood how protocol worked.

The Maharani usually spent the early morning hours, when it was cooler, with her children. There had been seven, two of whom had died in infancy. Parvati was the eldest, and there were two other daughters and two sons.

I'd heard tales that in the distant past female infants were not allowed to live, but the Princely families had daughters today, and like the Maharani, seemed to dote on them.

Parvati had given her Prince an heir a year after their wedding, and this little girl was the Maharani's first granddaughter. I could imagine the entire household staff eager to see and spoil the child. Private Dunn, who had ridden back with me, had seen her at a distance, and told me she was "quite the little dolly" in her multiple petticoats and gold bangles.

As I rode up the long drive toward the house, shaded by trees all the way to the main courtyard, for the eighth time I rearranged what I'd planned to say. Whatever I felt, I had to be diplomatic. The Prince was after all her son-in-law, Parvati's husband, and stuffed shirt or not, I had to be careful not to reflect in any way on his justice or his retainers. But I carried that bloody handkerchief and its contents with me, to show the Maharani.

From the start, the problem in this whole affair seemed to have been the senior official assigned to accompany Parvati on this visit. How well did the Maharani—or her daughter for that matter—know this man? And what did they think of him? How could I portray his role in all that had happened, and still make this matter seem to be a mistake that could easily be corrected, with no suggestion that he was inflexible and had an inflated sense of his own importance?

Major Dudley had ridden in shortly after Richard himself had come back—it was nearly dawn—and I hadn't had a chance to speak to him since he'd reported to Richard.

The broad steps leading up to the ornate garden door—where I'd been invited to come since first we'd met—were decorated with huge, ornate vases, where flowers grew, spilling over and scenting the air.

Usually a groom came running out to take my horse, but there was no one about, not even a gardener within sight. I dismounted at the block, tied up my horse, and went up the sweep of steps to pull the silk rope that served as a door knocker.

No one came to answer the summons. I waited a few minutes, then pulled the rope again. I knew someone had seen me. Nothing happened at the Palace without a hundred pairs of eyes watching every move.

Still no answer.

I stood there, gathering my wits. I hadn't expected to find the Maharani's door shut to me. And yet, when there was no answer to the third pull of the rope, I knew that I was no longer welcome here.

Gathering my dignity about me as best I could, I turned and walked with a straight back and a slow gait down the broad stairs and over to where my horse waited.

Mounting, I turned my back on the garden front of the Palace and rode sedately back the way I'd come. I could only hope my face was not pink from embarrassment.

Richard would have to come here in his official capacity, I told myself. She could not shut out the Regimental Colonel who protected her from the Frontier bandits.

I WENT STRAIGHT to Richard's office as soon as I reached the cantonment.

"What is it?" he said, as I was ushered through the door by the Corporal who guarded it.

"The Maharani has refused to see me."

"Has she indeed! I asked Dudley what the temperature was there, and he said they were greeted formally, the carts led around to the stables to be unloaded, and the Maharani's official, who came out to make a count of the carts and sign off on them, was rather stiff. Of course, this was the middle of the night. But Dudley and his men were not asked to dismount or shown any hospitality. When Dudley asked if the Princess had arrived safely and was all right, the man told him it was not his affair. Dudley took that to mean he was not to expect to interact with the household, and he and his men turned back toward the cantonment."

His was not a very forceful presence—I was aware of that. But he could hardly storm the Palace at that hour demanding to speak to someone in charge.

"I wonder how much Parvati knows about what happened there at the guesthouse. And if that man sent word with her staff that painted his own picture of what was going on." I bit my lip. "I should have gone with them, Richard. Instead of coming directly back here."

Richard shook his head. "They couldn't go any faster than the bullocks pulling the carts. You'd have been there in the middle of the night yourself, and the Maharani sound asleep in her bed."

"Yes, I know, I know. But if we can't see her—if we can't ask her help—what are we to do?"

"I'll make an official call this afternoon. At the front gates. Flags flying and a mounted troop at my back. We'll see how the Maharani deals with that."

Bess was disappointed that I hadn't seen Parvati or the baby. But she had other concerns too.

"Mummy, where is Simon? He's not in the barracks, he didn't ride in with my father, and he didn't return with Major Dudley. Where is he? Do you know? I was hoping to ask the Colonel Sahib, when he came home for his dinner, but he sent word that he was writing reports and would have something brought in from the officers' mess. Has something happened to Simon? Is that why he was writing reports all day?"

I was prepared for this too, but I hoped it would go better than the speech I was planning to give the Maharani.

"There was a problem at the guesthouse yesterday—or the night before, to be precise. Having to do with one of the Prince's people. Simon and several others have gone back to Rulumpur to sort it all out."

It was the story we'd agreed upon, Richard and I.

But Bess wasn't having it. "Dr. Broughton isn't here either. Has Simon been hurt? Was that what happened?"

"The last time I saw Simon, he was perfectly fine. Dr. Broughton went with me because we didn't wish to take officers who might be needed here. And you know how prickly the Princes can be about anything affecting their dignity. And a 19-gun salute princedom is often more prickly than most."

"The Maharani is a 21-gun salute state. And she's never been prickly."

"There's a first time for everything."

"I just don't see why Simon had to deal with the problem. He's got duties here."

"Darling, he isn't just out here to keep you from growing bored," I said, managing a smile. "He must obey orders as well."

She wasn't satisfied, and I noticed later that she was restless during our meal.

I wondered if perhaps she was growing too fond of Simon. But I told myself that she had all but grown up with him and had always treated him as a brother.

Richard came home briefly to change to his dress uniform, and I asked if I could accompany him to the Maharani's, even though I knew the answer.

"Dear girl, no," he said quietly. "I'll tell you everything. You know I will."

When he left, Bess asked, "Why is he calling on the Maharani in his official capacity?"

"I expect it's to greet the Prince's wife. Parvati has status now—she's not just a friend and playmate."

"I suppose." Clearly at loose ends, she watched her father striding across the parade ground toward his office.

"Didn't a packet of new sheet music arrive last week? Have you mastered all of the pieces?"

"I'm just not in the mood to play. I was writing a letter to Cousin Melinda, and I expect I ought to finish that."

I found it just as hard to sit and do nothing while I awaited Richard's return. Instead, I put a scarf over my hair and began to dust and clean my sitting room. That brought our housekeeper rushing in to take the feather dusters away from me, scolding me for not summoning her and insisting she would see to it at once. I took a turn in the gardens, but as the dry season was coming to its end, so were the blooms on the flowers. The afternoon seemed to crawl by.

And then I heard the horses coming in, and I knew Richard was back. But he didn't come at once to the house, and shortly afterward, I saw a mounted runner set out at a gallop.

That meant a telegram was being sent.

An ominous sign . . .

A few minutes later, one of the Privates came to ask me to meet the Colonel in his office, and I knew I'd been right. There was more trouble than I'd anticipated.

I found my hat against the sun, and my parasol, and set out to accompany the young man.

Richard was waiting for me.

"It's worse than we thought," he said bluntly as he shut the door to his office and handed me to a chair.

"Did you see the Maharani?" I asked, unable to wait another minute.

"Yes. You'd have thought we had never spent five minutes in her company before. I was taken to a formal audience chamber, and she came in at her regal best. I asked after her daughter, and she was frosty. And so I played the same card, and told her that I was there on official business, asking politely but coldly for any information she or her daughter had regarding events at the guesthouse."

He paused, staring out the window at a swirl of dust racing across the parade grounds. "She told me that she was quite surprised when her daughter arrived with such a small escort and none of her baggage. But a letter handed to her from the Prince's senior official reported that he had sent her posthaste to the safety of the Palace, because he feared for her life."

"*What?* Richard—Simon told Dr. Broughton something about that, but I took it to mean that the minister was exaggerating to save face. As far as I know—and Lieutenant Hayes knew—she wasn't aware of that poor man's death. I mean to say, while it marred her homecoming, a little, to arrive without her full escort, she herself was never in any danger."

"I accept that, and you accept it. But the Maharani showed me the letter. My written Hindi is rusty, but I could read it well enough to know she was telling the truth."

"But who would wish to kill Parvati? She's the Prince's wife, yes, but she has no—no *political* importance. She's never been a threat to anyone." I took a deep breath, forcing myself to think clearly. "He wrote that, Richard, to excuse the helter-skelter way she'd arrived at her mother's home. That's what this is about."

He was frowning. "I don't think so. Well, perhaps partly, yes, I expect you're right. But there's more to it than covering his incompetence. Whatever is going on here, whatever really happened in that compound in the middle of the night, the man is worried. And Simon is going to be his scapegoat. But for what?"

"Did you at least speak to Parvati?"

"No. The Maharani told me she was fatigued from her travels. And that she was resting."

"You sent a telegram as soon as you got back from the Palace. Why?"

He reached out and took my hand. "I told the Prince himself that I'd be arriving as soon as possible. And that I would hold him officially responsible for anything that happened to my Sergeant Major. And that a copy of that telegram was being sent to Calcutta."

"Will he listen?"

"If he doesn't, I'll go directly to Calcutta." But that was all the way across the continent of India. "Pack as lightly as you can. We leave at dawn tomorrow." He glanced toward his desk. "I shouldn't leave now, given the situation out there at the Pass. But that will have to wait. Dudley can hold the fort. And I'll see that orders are left for any contingency."

"I'll see to your valise as well," I told him, rising. "But what shall I tell Bess? She's nearly fourteen, Richard, and she's already asking about Simon."

"God help me, I don't know."

As I WAS packing, Bess came in.

I took a deep breath and turned to her. "I must tell you something, Bess." I sat down on the bed and drew her down to sit beside me. "Something happened as the Princess's entourage spent the night at the guesthouse. You know the one—we've stopped there ourselves."

I told her how one of the bullock cart men had gone to see to his wagon, and apparently found someone breaking into it. "When the body was found, a casket lay beside him, upside down and empty. When they went looking for the killer, they discovered that Simon had one of the baby's rattles in his saddlebags and what appeared to be some of the money from the broken box. He's been taken back to the Prince's Palace to explain what happened." It was the best I could do.

"If that were all," she replied, "you and the Colonel Sahib wouldn't be packing to go after him. Have they arrested *him*? But that's ridiculous—Simon isn't a thief."

Bess was levelheaded and intelligent. I couldn't lie to her, even to protect her.

Before I could answer her, she went on. "Is that why you went on your own to call on the Maharani? To speak to Parvati? What did she have to say? I thought she liked Simon?"

"It's a tangle, darling. Even I don't know what's happening. That's why your father is going himself to try to sort it out." Trying for a lighter note, I added, "You needn't worry about Simon. It's the Prince who will need your pity, once the Colonel Sahib has stormed his Palace."

I'd meant for her to smile, and she did, but turning quickly, she said, "I'll pack my things—I'm going with you."

I scrambled for a way to keep her here. "No, wait—I haven't been able to speak to the Maharani or Parvati. That's your task, darling, to find a way to visit with Parvati. We need to know what she can tell us about this matter. Whatever you learn, you must send us a telegram. Major Dudley will see to it. Anything that will help. Can you do that?"

Her face fell. "If you think that's the best way to help Simon . . ."

"They won't let me through the door, Bess. But you could find Parvati in the gardens—somehow—and that would be the most tremendous help."

"I wish Cousin Melinda was here. She knows quite a few of the Princes, I think. She could bring pressure to bear on Parvati's husband."

"We've been told the King has died. It hasn't been verified, so it's best not to spread rumors. If it's true, Melinda will want to be in London. She knew him fairly well." Not, I thought, in the way so many women did, but as a friend.

"She'd be here for Simon, if she could."

"She doesn't know him, Bess. I don't think they've ever met."

"I've written to her about him. About how much I like him, and how close he is to you and the Colonel Sahib."

"Have you indeed?" I replied, fair flummoxed, as our cook at home would have put it. "And—um—what has she had to say about that?"

"She wrote that friendships are to be valued. And she looks forward to meeting him one day." She considered that, head to one side. "I've thought about that. I think they would be great friends."

"And why is that?"

"Because of what he's done with his career. That's why she's so fond of my father. I think the Colonel Sahib reminds her of her late husband. She told me once he was a fine officer."

"Simon isn't an officer."

"He could have been. I know my father asked him several times if he'd like to go back to England to Sandhurst."

I went back to my packing. "Yes, of course. Will you be all right on your own, here? And you'll take an escort when you go to the Palace? Even though you must leave them well outside the gates?"

"You know I will."

We talked about several household matters as I finished my packing and turned to Richard's. I was worried about leaving her alone—even though there was a regiment at our doorstep.

And then, at six o'clock in the morning, the horses were brought around, and we rode away, Bess standing by the compound gate waving to us. She had given me a letter to pass on to Simon.

I wasn't even certain we would be allowed to see him . . .

MOST OF THE wealthier Princes had private trains. Far more elegant and running on their schedule, not ours. We had to wait for the morning train to Lahore, and then transfer to another for Delhi, and then back again to Rulumpur on a spur line, arriving in the evening of the third day. The Prince's train would have gone directly.

That meant the Prince's man would have been days ahead of us. And who knew what mischief he'd done with such a head start.

Richard was edgy, sometimes leaving our first-class compart-
ment to walk the length of the train and back again. I pretended to
be far calmer than I was. But by the time we pulled into the station
below the Palace at Rulumpur, we were thoroughly sick of travel
and worried beyond words.

We were taken by sedan chair to the residence set aside for
visiting potentates, viceregal guests, and other visitors who had no
claim to stay in the Palace itself. It sat on the edge of a large lake,
shimmering in the moonlight as we came past. I looked up at the
enormous, rambling facade and wondered if somewhere behind
all those elegant windows and arches and balconies Simon was
being kept in some sort of Princely dungeon. Shaking myself, I
smiled at the staff as we were greeted and shown to our quarters.

When our luggage was delivered and we'd declined staff help in
unpacking, I stood in the middle of the ornately decorated room
and for the second time since all this had begun, I wanted to cry.

Instead, I said to Richard, "Do you think you'll be granted an
audience?"

"I expect the Prince will have to give me one. If only to keep me
from reporting him to the Governor-General."

There was a knock at the door, and two men in livery brought
in a table with fruit and sweetmeats and tea to welcome us. And
there was as well an envelope, heavy stationery embossed with the
Prince's seal.

We waited for the men to retire, and then Richard picked it up,
used one of the table knives to slit it open, and drew out the single
sheet.

"Tomorrow morning at ten. I have an audience then."

"I want to be there."

"Darling, you can't. This is addressed only to me."

"I'll go even if I must wait in an antechamber—"

There was another knock at the door, and when Lieutenant Hayes stepped into the room, I could see by the look on his face that the news was *not* good. Lines that I didn't remember were there around his mouth, and under his eyes were dark circles from the strain he'd been under.

Richard greeted him, asked him to sit, and then said, "What is the news?"

"The trial was yesterday, ending this morning in sentencing." He glanced at me, as if he wished himself anywhere but here.

"What do you mean, the sentencing?" I asked, as Richard retorted, "There shouldn't have been a trial before I got here."

"I did my best," Lieutenant Hayes said grimly. "Believe me, I gave them to understand that there would be serious repercussions."

"The sentence?" I said again.

Lieutenant Hayes looked down at his hands. "He's sentenced to hang at dawn, in two days' time."

I thought my heart would stop, and Richard's face went white, then anger flooded it with color again. He was on his feet, heading for the door, when Lieutenant Hayes said, "Sir—no, you mustn't—not tonight. Please?"

Richard stopped. "No. Of course, you're right. What the hell were the charges? And who were the witnesses? What sort of trial was it?" He came back and sat down, taking my hand in his. Mine was shaking, and the warmth of his seemed to start me breathing again.

"All proper enough, I expect. But—there were—he had an affidavit. Well, a witnessed statement. It was from the ayah who was there in the carriage with the child. When Simon stopped by the carriage—you know about that rattle? Yes. When he stopped by the carriage, the ayah, the nursemaid, stated that he made unwelcomed advances toward the Princess. And when she sent him away, the ayah heard him mutter that he'd see her dead if he couldn't have her."

"*What?*" I said, as Richard exclaimed, "That's rot."

I added, "I'd no more believe that of Simon than I would of Richard, here."

"Nor I," Hayes said wretchedly. "But why would she say these things? What purpose did she have for lying? I can't fathom it. Nothing was said about this when we gathered in that room at the guesthouse. And he'd already sent the Princess on her way to her mother's—we couldn't have questioned her if we'd wanted to, without going after her."

I understood then, why I had not been welcomed at the Maharani's Palace. She must have known that Simon had once thought he was in love with her daughter. I hadn't told her, of course, but perhaps Parvati had had feelings that worried her mother. And so the ayah's evidence might have been believed. But—what about the Princess herself? Why had she let such a lie stand? Why hadn't she stopped this madness by telling her mother and her husband that the woman was lying?

Then I remembered, the nursemaid was the Prince's servant— she ran the royal nursery. And she would do as he asked—as his minister asked—including lying about what had been said between Simon and Parvati.

But what had that minister to gain by accusing Simon of such crimes? Was he using a British soldier to further some scheme of his own? Some ambition for more authority at Court?

Oh, God, I thought. *If I'd known—I would have found a way into that Palace—I would have got the truth out of them, somehow.*

I'd heard stories about how the Princes would have a servant beaten in place of their sons, who couldn't be touched in spite of their misbehavior. I felt like beating the ayah, for the truth. To make her tell me why she had thrown Simon to the wolves.

Trying to calm down, I reminded myself that the woman might have been forced to write such a statement. If that were the case, the Maharani would surely have learned the truth by now? Or was she also unaware of what his minister was up to?

Richard was demanding to know more about the trial, if an appeal was allowed, if the sentence could be changed for any reason.

The Lieutenant was shaking his head. "There's no appeal. None. I've pounded on doors, asking."

"Where is Simon?"

He took a long breath. "We haven't been able to see him. Not since he was led away. I'm told the Prince was furious—he's a jealous man, apparently. Well, she's quite pretty, of course, and from what I've gathered here and there, she's given him no reason for doubting her. It's odd, you know. He's a Prince—he has everything a man could possibly want. A lovely wife, son, a daughter." He gestured around him. "All this—power and money and position—yet he's doubtful of himself. I don't understand it."

Richard said, "Not too surprising. He's been told all his life, from the moment he was born, that he was the center of the universe. Perhaps he's learned the truth."

"Well, no. He was the second son, I'm told. His elder brother died of cholera when he was five or six."

"All the more reason to feel he wasn't born to rule. Will they allow me to see Simon—speak to him in private?"

Lieutenant Hayes sighed. "I don't think so, sir. They have refused us. Even the doctor hasn't been allowed to see the Sergeant Major. He was told that the Prince's physician will deal with any health issues that might arise."

Richard was pacing the floor. Thinking hard. "Was it a public trial?"

"No. Given the charges, I expect—but it was conducted just as it would have been in public. As far as I could tell. Simon was represented, but the man had very little to say. Simon was asked how he pleaded, and he told them 'Not Guilty.' When asked why he'd threatened the Princess, he answered that he'd done no such thing. He had spoken to her as a childhood friend, pleased to see her return to her mother's with her own daughter, and glad to see her happy. He had searched for the rattle because the little girl was restless in the heat and with the motion of the carriage, and he had felt sorry for her."

"There was no deposition from the Princess?"

"No. Unless she'd been a party to what was happening, she'd have been kept out of it."

"What about the murder and the theft of the items in the little casket? Why, if Simon was interested in the Princess, had he committed those crimes?"

"Apparently he was looking for money to bribe her servants and take her away."

Richard swore, and didn't apologize. I felt like swearing as well.

"The casket he'd broken into," I said, "was hardly going to keep a Princess in the life she'd been accustomed to living."

"Apparently he'd been interrupted in his search," the Lieutenant replied.

"It's all so—so neat and tidy," I said. "Except that it isn't the sort of thing Simon would do."

"Perhaps Simon was the only member of the Army, aside from the Lieutenant here, who had been seen speaking to the Princess," Richard said. "And it would have been difficult to accuse Hayes instead, because it was his duty to see to her comfort and safety."

"Come to that," the Lieutenant responded, "the Prince's man saw to it that I greeted her on arrival, in the name of our Regiment, that I asked if the rooms in the guesthouse were to her liking, and that was all."

We talked for almost another hour. But we were no wiser then than when the Lieutenant had walked in our door. When he left, Richard went to the untouched table of food and poured himself a stiff whiskey.

"What are we to do?" I asked quietly. "We can't let him hang!"

He came to sit down next to me, keeping his voice low. Who knew how many ears this guesthouse had? "You are going to the Palace after all. And while I am being received by the Prince, you will be escorted to the zenana. I will wager you will learn more there than I shall in the audience. Something's wrong, Clarissa, and we are going to get to the bottom of it."

Shaken out of my shock, I smiled. "Of course. And I've brought just the dress to wear."

He laughed then. "I'm sure you did." The laugh faded. "We must get some rest. Tomorrow will be a harrowing day. But Simon is coming back with us if I must break him out myself."

AT THE APPOINTED hour we were driven up to the Palace in one of the Prince's motorcars. Most of the Princes had gone mad for them. And this Rolls was in the royal blue of the Prince's house, although there was no leather in the motorcar, the seats being covered in French petit point, while polished wood paneling replaced any other bits that would have been leather. Cows, of course, are sacred in India. The ceiling was covered in cream watered silk.

We were handed from staff to staff—Richard had to relinquish his dress sword along the way—and finally found ourselves in the elegant room where the Prince received guests of our status. It was designed to impress, in royal blue and silver.

He kept us waiting for fifteen minutes, then came in with his staff around him. There was the Dewan, his equivalent of a prime minister, his Secretary, a formidable man with graying hair, and the British Secretary in charge of Rulumpur.

The Prince was not very tall, reminding me of Edward—he must be Prince of Wales now, I realized, as his father had become King George V. We'd seen the black bordered announcements of Edward VII's death in all the Delhi newspapers. That, it had turned out, was true.

Slim and wearing glasses, the Prince looked more like a studious Oxford man than the head of a 19-gun salute Princely state, in spite of his satin coat and formal turban. The rope of large black pearls around his neck matched the black armband he wore in mourning for the King.

His manner toward us was cold, while Richard was as formal as the Governor-General himself could be on occasion. And that seemed to daunt the Prince.

"We've come to learn why one of my men, a respected member of the British Army, was tried and found guilty of charges that make no sense. I would be grateful if you would explain the circumstances to me."

"My mother would be glad to entertain your lady wife in the zenana," he replied.

And someone appeared as if by magic to conduct me there. I felt as if I'd abandoned Richard, in a way, but I knew he was right. I could do more good elsewhere.

We went through a dozen passages into a part of the Palace that belonged to the women of the family. The Prince hadn't, to my knowledge, taken a second wife—that was going out of fashion— but the zenana was full of women.

I was introduced to the Rajmata, his widowed mother, then to *her* mother, and to several aunts who were visiting, and then to the Prince's other mothers, the two women his father had married after his senior wife.

I was beginning to wish I'd brought Bess with me. She might have distracted some of them.

Smiling, the Rajmata ordered refreshments, and in one corner of the room, someone behind a screen began playing a musical instrument.

When the formalities had been dealt with and we were all seated comfortably on an array of silk cushions, the Prince's mother asked what brought me to visit here.

"My husband, the Colonel of the Regiment, and I are very concerned about one of my husband's men. He has been accused of serious crimes. We have reason to believe that he is not guilty— that a serious mistake has been made."

I had carried a large handbag with me, and I reached inside it. Bringing out the roll of bloody silk handkerchief, with the little purse of rupees and the gold chain, I laid them out on the floor, adding the knife last.

There were gasps and little cries as the women leaned forward to stare at what I had spread out before them.

The Rajmata said, "Have these been shown to my son?"

"Not yet, Your Highness. I was present when these were discovered." I explained how that had happened, and she listened closely.

An aunt said, "Who was this murdered man?"

"He was a driver of a bullock cart," I said.

"Lower caste, then." The grandmother.

"Yes, Your Highness. It was thought he interrupted his killer rifling one of the carts. But my husband's soldiers don't carry silk handkerchiefs, only cotton or linen ones. And this is not the sort of knife they carry." I pointed to the handle. "It is like so many in the bazaar, and there is a carving of Ganesh in the handle. What's more, my husband's soldiers would never have insulted the Princess. The Maharani, her mother, has been a guest in our home any number of times, and we have been guests of hers."

"Who has said she was insulted? The Princess?"

"I have been unable to speak to her about this. The accuser is her child's ayah. Why she should wish to accuse one of my husband's men is a mystery. I should like to know more about this woman."

There was some discussion among the ladies. I could follow most of it, and the gist was, the child's nursemaid had come to Rulumpur with the most junior wife of the late Rajah, then been put in charge of the nursery.

That most junior wife spoke up then. "My mother chose her to accompany me. She had saved my sister who had fallen ill of cholera, nursing her day and night, when the doctors had given up all hope. And she lived. It was hoped that this woman would save my children if one fell ill."

I sipped the cool drink I'd been given—it tasted of apricots and honey—and then asked, "And she was also chosen to accompany the Princess?"

The grandmother spoke then. "It is not a good time of year to travel. Children can fall ill. The Princess's little daughter is much loved here."

I tried another tack. "Why did the Princess decide to travel this month?"

There was a long silence. And then the Rajmata said, "She and my son the Prince had a falling-out."

Oh, dear.

One of the aunts added, "We should have left for the hill country three weeks ago. But the Prince does not wish to leave without his wife. And Parvati did not wish to go."

"May I ask why they had a falling-out?"

Again there was some discussion, and finally I was told.

"They have one son. The Prince wishes to send him to England to study. As he did in his own youth. He believes that we must learn about England. Not just from the Resident, but from our own experience. The Princess felt the boy was still too young. And she did not care for the people who would have been given the charge of him while he was abroad. She wanted him to study in Mysore, where state administration is an art."

I was doing some rapid arithmetic in my head.

The Prince and his wife were fighting over their children— she'd left for a visit to her mother, never mind the time of year, and most likely intended to stay for a while. And the ayah, the nursemaid, would surely have known this, if she lived here in the zenana. But why would she use this against Simon Brandon? To bring the Prince and Princess back together? Had she even been put up to this by one of these women? I wouldn't put it past the

Rajmata—she had very good reasons for keeping her son and his wife happy together, at least in public. The Maharani outranked her. It would be a reflection on her son that he couldn't keep his wife at home. Still, the Prince *could* put Parvati away, if there was a very good reason, then marry again. And Simon might have unwittingly given the ayah an opportunity to present the Prince with that reason. But who then had killed the bullock cart driver?

Palace intrigue didn't explain murder, did it? Two and two were not adding up to four.

Oh, dear.

I touched the items on the floor in front of me, spread out on the stained square of silk. "I have trusted Simon Brandon with my own daughter. To teach her to ride and shoot, to accompany her when she goes beyond the boundaries of the cantonment. I would have trusted him with the Maharani's daughter. He and the other soldiers were chosen as her escort because they had impeccable records. I have not known him to be a violent man. The thing is, if he is executed for something he did not do, it will alienate the Army, it will alienate the Maharani, and it will alienate the Governor-General in Calcutta. I can understand that the Prince must feel his dignity has been attacked, and his wife insulted. He has a reputation for being a good and fair man. Perhaps *we* could find a face-saving solution that would satisfy all parties."

One of the aunts opened her mouth to speak, and thought better of it. The Prince's mother hadn't answered me.

When she did, it was unexpected. "This man has been found guilty in a fair trial."

"Was it fair? His commanding officer was not present. The officers who *were* here were not allowed to question him in order to prepare a defense. We do not know what the Princess heard. We only have the word of a nursemaid."

The Rajmata gestured to the things on the handkerchief. "Perhaps this was left for you to find, because he was taken into custody before he could retrieve it."

I touched the little purse, and the gold chain. "If I were planning to take your daughter and harm her, I would need more than this to help me to escape afterward. That cart was filled with far more than this paltry sum."

"He did not have time to find more. Because he was interrupted."

I smiled. "It is my understanding that the man who owned the cart was found well over an hour later, when next the guard came by on his rounds. His killer could have taken what he pleased in that space of time. Perhaps it wasn't the treasure he wanted, perhaps it was to *appear* to be a theft, so that there seemed to be a reason for the murder. Perhaps the ayah knows who planned this, and blamed my husband's soldier to cover that death."

The Rajmata stared at me. "You are accusing us in this matter."

"No, Your Highness. I am seeking the truth. If my husband is convinced that his soldier didn't commit any crime and did not insult the Princess he was there to protect, then what really happened at that guesthouse? Your son's good name is just as much at risk as Sergeant Major Brandon's. He would not wish it to be said that he put an innocent man to death."

I'd pushed too far. In my need to do something, I'd gone about it the wrong way.

She rose, an imposing figure. "Take these things you have brought here and leave."

I did just that, and as I rose to my feet, I said, "We are both mothers, Your Highness. We will do anything to protect our families. But Sergeant Major Brandon's mother isn't here to speak in his place. I have tried to speak for her."

And with the proper salaams, I left the zenana, my heart in my shoes.

I SAT IN an antechamber for a quarter of an hour before Richard came out of the audience chamber, his expression grim.

Without a word, I joined him, and we left the Palace, where the motorcar waited to convey us to the guesthouse. But when the motorcar had left us at the door, Richard said, "Let's walk."

We found a small pavilion overlooking the lake where we could be private, and Richard said trenchantly, "I got nowhere."

I waited as he collected himself. "The Dewan is a Brahmin, the Resident is a man with no backbone. And the Prince is convinced that his wife was in grave danger. I doubt he cares one whit about the dead man. Somehow he's been led to believe that if Simon had managed to return that golden rattle to Parvati, he would have taken her away or killed her outright."

I didn't say anything. I was too numb. A little breeze rippled the surface of the water, and the image of the Palace shivered in the sunlight.

"The trial was held on a day that the Prince's advisor told him was auspicious. And the sentence will be carried out on an auspicious day as well. Dear God!"

"Will they let you see him? *Richard?*"

"On the last morning."

I closed my eyes.

"I told the Prince that the Governor-General would see him deposed if he refused the decency of comforting an innocent man."

"You haven't given up!"

"No. God, no. I'm sending a telegram to Minto in Calcutta asking for a pardon. And I'm meeting with the Resident, to force him to find some backbone. If it had only been the murder of a poor carter, who wasn't one of the Prince's subjects, if it had been theft of a few rupees and a gold chain, we might have won. But this threat to the Prince's wife can't be erased. What I can't begin to understand is why the nursemaid reported such a thing. What could Simon have said to make anyone believe he could harm Parvati? Who put the ayah up to that? What does anyone have to gain by this madness?"

"In the zenana, they seemed to think the nursemaid was telling the truth. But I think—I believe—that the Prince's man had something to do with convincing everyone of that. Why would a lowly nursemaid take it upon herself to lie? *Someone* is behind this, Richard. And is that person trying to bring the Prince and his wife back together? Or to give him an acceptable reason for him to put her aside? Why didn't Parvati herself speak up? She *knew* Simon!"

I told him what had happened there in the zenana.

And afterward we walked to the railway station, down the hill, and through the crowded streets, rather than ask someone from the hotel to send the telegram for us.

The railways of India belong to the Government, the Princes have no authority over them.

We could be sure that any telegram sent from there would safely reach its destination. Richard had already decided what he would say, and he wrote out his lengthy message without hesitation. We stood there, watching, until it had actually been sent, then gave the stationmaster the name of our hotel, for any reply.

We took a rickshaw back up the hill, too distraught to enjoy the colorful crowds heading for the shops and the bazaars, and went directly to our rooms.

It wasn't long before Lieutenant Hayes, Dr. Broughton, and the adjutant came to our door to ask for news.

Watching the hope fade from their faces as Richard told them what had transpired made events even more real for me. I sat there, my cup of tea untouched, as they made suggestion after suggestion, trying to find any solution to what was going to happen—in two days' time.

If it had been my own child sitting in that cell, I couldn't have felt more wretched. And I knew Richard felt the same. Finally, to give us a little peace, he sent the three men to find out what they could about the ayah and the Prince's man who had been with the caravan. He was, I'd learned, a minor state minister, which is why he had the ear of the Prince and we did not. Lieutenant Hayes was of the opinion the man was ambitious, looking to climb the political ladder, so to speak, any way he could.

It gave them something to do, a sense of purpose, which they needed badly. And Richard sent a request to the Palace for a second audience.

That went about as well as the first.

The Prince put it best. "This man you claim is innocent has threatened my wife, and I have lost face with my mother-in-law because I failed to protect Parvati. She will not be safe until he is dead."

The Dewan, regarding us with cold eyes, said, "You say you

know this man. But he is of the ranks, and should have known better than to approach the Princess. Yet he did. What other purpose could it have been, than to threaten her?"

"My daughter," I said, "often visited Parvati at her mother's home. Simon was often Bess's escort to and from the Palace. If he'd had designs on the Princess, he could have carried them out then and there. Here he was in the midst of a well-guarded caravan. Why not wait until the Princess was back at home with her mother?"

"He is young. He has not learned restraint in matters such as this. It does you honor to fight for one of your own, but here your case is without merit."

RICHARD HAD NO better luck seeing the Resident, a Mr. Aylesford, later in the evening.

This was, we discovered, his first posting with a Prince of a 19-gun salute. He'd spent much of his career with a Chief of a 5-gun salute, was promoted from there to a Prince with 10 guns. He wanted nothing to do with any problems that would see him removed from the Prince's household and demoted.

"You're the Government's man on the ground, here. You have the authority to ask that his ruling be reexamined," Richard pointed out.

"But this has to do with his wife, you see," the Resident replied. "That's a gray area, and we try not to involve ourselves in domestic matters. There is never a happy result."

"Once a man's life has been taken, there is no turning back. I have written to the Governor-General, Lord Minto, requesting his intercession. It will not look very good for your record if he finds that you've allowed the execution of an innocent man."

That flustered him. But he regained a little of his poise as he said, "I have it on good authority that Lord Minto is not in Calcutta. He's in Delhi, arranging a suitable service to mark the King's passing."

We left soon after. And Richard went back to the telegraph office in the railway station to send another telegram, this time to Delhi.

Another restless, sleepless night passed. I could hardly swallow food, but made myself eat a little to keep from falling ill.

At ten o'clock in the morning, I couldn't stand it any longer. "I'm going back to the zenana. I want to speak to the Rajmata."

"I'll escort you."

And so we found ourselves back at the Palace once more. I asked to be taken to the zenana, and after a few minutes, an escort arrived to take me there.

But at the door, I was told that the ladies did not wish to receive me.

There was no appeal.

I had to follow my escort back to the antechamber where Richard waited.

We even went to the police station, where I told the man in charge that I was Sergeant Major Brandon's mother and that I wished to see him.

We were turned away.

When we reached the hotel again, I asked Richard to pour me a small whiskey as well. I felt hollow inside.

In less than twenty-four hours, Simon would hang.

WE WENT BACK to the pavilion in spite of the day's heat, and sat there in wounded silence. We had found a message ordering us to present ourselves at the prison gates at 4:00 a.m. if we wished to speak to the prisoner. We had also gone back to the telegraph office to ask if any replies to our earlier telegrams had been received. They had not.

At one point, Richard said, "I won't let him hang. I'll kill him myself first."

"They'll search us for weapons—"

He pulled out a small revolver. "It isn't very accurate at any distance, but at point-blank range, it will do. If you are on the verge of fainting, and I must support you, it's possible that they'll miss finding it."

I swallowed hard. "It won't be that far from the truth. But I won't leave, Richard. No matter what, I won't leave."

As the sun went down, casting long rays of light reflecting off the dust motes in the air, we turned back to the guesthouse.

We had just reached the main door when someone called out to Richard.

"Colonel Crawford? Sir—?"

We turned, and saw that it was the clerk from the telegraph office.

"I was just at the guesthouse, looking for you. This came in a quarter of an hour ago."

He handed Richard an envelope, touched his cap, and was gone down the street on an aged bicycle.

Richard was about to tear it open.

"Not here," I said quickly, and we hurried up the stairs to our room. There, the door closed behind Richard, he opened the telegram and pulled out the sheet.

His face fell as I watched.

"He refused?" I whispered, knowing it was our last hope.

Richard held out the telegram. "It's not from Minto. It's from Bess."

I took it and read it.

Mother, something about the ayah's brother. Find out.

It took me a moment to remember that I'd asked Bess to speak to Parvati, if she could.

Was this all that she had managed to learn?

I felt ill.

Still, I said to Richard, "I'm going back to the zenana."

"They won't receive you."

"They will, if I have to break down the door. At least I won't be sitting here watching the hands on that clock." I pointed to the mantel where a French ormolu clock, bracketed by even more ornate candlesticks, the base held up by the trunks of gold elephants, ticked away the time.

We hurried to the Palace. The gates had closed at dusk, and Richard had to demand to see the officer of the guard.

"It's an urgent matter," I said as he came to see what the fuss was all about.

"I've just received a telegram regarding the Maharani, the Princess's mother. I must speak to the Rajmata at once."

"What is this urgent matter?" the officer demanded.

"It is zenana business."

He dithered for a moment, then ordered the smaller gate to be opened, and I was admitted. Richard was asked to wait outside.

I shot him a glance full of hope, then followed the guard to another antechamber, and then the same escort came to take me to the zenana.

Once more I was told that they were not receiving guests.

I said, "Please tell the Rajmata that this is an urgent message regarding the ayah who accompanied the Princess to her mother's house."

The young woman who had sent me away before left me standing there, and a few minutes later she was back.

"The Rajmata is not receiving visitors."

I argued for nearly ten minutes, and then was told in no uncertain terms that I must leave.

I turned to my escort. "If they refuse to speak to me, I wish to speak to the Prince."

"He is at his dinner and has guests."

"I don't wish to disturb his guests, but it is imperative that I see him."

But it was clear that orders had been given.

I followed my escort, desperately trying to find another approach. I was just about to lie and tell anyone who would listen that the Governor-General had responded to our telegram when a door opened down the passage, and a woman said, "Leave her. I will see that she is taken to the door."

I stepped into the antechamber—the Palace appeared to have dozens of them—and found myself face-to-face with one of the late Prince's junior wives. I remembered her from my earlier visit.

Finding my tongue, I said, "I am grateful for your seeing me—"

But she politely cut me short. "What is it about the ayah to the Princess's daughter?"

"I understand she has a brother—" I began.

"Had," the woman told me. She had on the most beautiful sari, I thought in one part of my mind. The color of apricots with a gold fringe . . .

"What do you mean, *had*?"

"He was killed when he was twelve."

"I'm sorry—" This was going nowhere. But I changed my disappointment to polite concern, "I am sorry to hear it."

"A bullock cart was passing. She was sixteen—she saw it all. A heavy load came loose from the cart and fell on him. He died in great pain hours later. I brought her with me when I was married to the Prince's father. To take her away from her memories. I was young myself, and had a tender heart. It was allowed because she was a known healer."

I was suddenly alert. "What happened? It was an accident, surely."

"The man with the cart ran away. He was never found. She has been searching for him all her life. She was told that someone hadn't secured the load well enough. Still, she blamed him."

My throat was dry. "Do—do you think she found him? Among the bullock cart drivers taking the Princess to her mother's house?" I hadn't seen the dead man's body. I couldn't know how old he was.

The late Prince's junior wife was silent for a moment. I thought she was weighing just how much to tell me. Then she said, "I recognized the knife, you see. It was her brother's. She had kept it, to kill the man who had killed him."

She had done just that—and to protect herself, she had lied about Simon.

It was bad manners, but I had to sit down in the nearest chair. My legs didn't seem to want to hold me. Finally I said, "There is a man who is going to die in a matter of hours for a crime he didn't commit. Will you let that happen?"

"I cannot stop it."

"But you must!" I stood up again, facing her. Fighting for this last chance. "There has to be a way. Otherwise, why did you tell me?"

"It is the truth. But there are other issues here. She is in the Princess's retinue. It will not look well to have her arrested for this crime."

"She *lied*. Don't you see? She lied to everyone. To the Prince's minister—to the Maharani. And she did this knowing she would be believed. She is sending a man to the gallows who had nothing to do with her brother's death. She had seen him speak to the Princess. And she twisted his words on purpose." When she said nothing, I went on. "He will die in a very few hours. I have been given permission to watch this man die, because he deserves to know that we believe in him, the people who know him best. That we have fought until the very end to save him. And you have that power."

"There is nothing I can do."

Well, there was.

I said, "If your prisoner dies in spite of all you have told me, I will stop in Delhi on my way back to the Regiment. And I shall tell anyone who will listen what you have done here. The newspapers, the Governor-General. I will see that that woman is taken from the Princess's retinue and made to stand trial. And I will be a witness at that trial. By the time I have finished, she will be sentenced for murder, and the good name of this Princely state will be ruined forever."

"You cannot do this. The Prince now believes that it is because of this man that the Princess has left him. Not the education of his son."

"Oh, dear God," I said, exasperated. "This isn't the Middle Ages. This may be a 19-gun salute state, but when I am finished, the British Government will depose the Prince and take over Rulumpur permanently. I too have friends in high places, in London, and this will be done. I promise you."

If Melinda couldn't do it, I'd appeal to the King. The new King. He was said to be a serious family man, unlike his father. He might well listen. The newspapers surely would. Simon would be dead, but I would see that his name was cleared.

"I suggest you return to the zenana, and discuss this with the Rajmata. If that young man is hanged at dawn, you will find your-selves paying dearly for his death." I gestured to the elegant deco-rations of this little room. "I understand the Taj Hotel in Bombay is very fine. Perhaps none of you will miss the Palace too much."

And I turned, opened the door, and walked out.

As soon as I did, I realized my anguish had got the better of me, and I might just have finished any real hope Simon had.

But it was too late. I'd wagered his life against their future. And I'd meant every word.

The escort was still there. I was led back to where Richard was waiting. And I said in the hearing of the escort, "I have delivered an ultimatum. I intend to sit here until there is an answer."

And I sat down.

IT WAS THREE in the morning when we walked back to the guest-house. There had been no word from the Rajmata or the Prince.

There were no telegrams at the guesthouse, and none that was waiting to be delivered. We walked on to the prison. My stomach was in knots.

Richard said, "You did all you could."

"I shouldn't have lost my temper and threatened them. But that's what they fear most—being deposed by the Government and their estates absorbed. I've heard the Maharani speak about this. It's very real. Even now, when a Prince dies, his heir must be reported to the Governor-General, and his approval given." I looked up at Richard. His face was haggard. "It was the only weapon I possessed."

We had reached the prison. Richard identified us and we were allowed to enter, and then we were left in the warder's office until it was time.

"If you shoot Simon, they will hang you," I said into the heavy silence.

"I know."

"Let me do it. I have a better chance of surviving."

"No."

I couldn't speak for the tightness in my throat.

The door opened, and the head warder stood there. "You will come with me."

I won't cry, I told myself fiercely. *Whatever happens, I won't cry. Not here . . .*

We followed him into the corridor, and he turned back toward the gates.

"No—" Richard said.

"The matter is finished."

Beside me, Richard swore in despair.

"The Prince—we were *promised*," I said. Was this how the Prince intended to punish us? By taking away our last chance to see Simon? To do what had to be done?

He opened the last door. "Go," he said.

There was nothing more to be done. We stumbled blindly across the threshold in a state of shock, and the door was shut behind us.

"This way," Richard said, his voice unrecognizable, and we walked down the last corridor, and the guards at the gate opened it to usher us out. Dawn was just breaking and the heat was like a wall. "It isn't the end, Clarissa, I swear to you—"

A tall figure stepped out of the shadows beside the gate.

"How soon can we leave?" Simon asked. "I don't know why they let me go, but I'd prefer to put as much distance as I can between us and this place."

He was wearing his uniform, filthy now, and he looked on the brink of exhaustion. I thought it was willpower alone that kept him on his feet.

Turning to me, he said, "I don't know how you managed it. But I owe you—I can never repay—" He stopped, unable to go on.

I wanted to reach out, touch him, be certain he was really there.

But the English have a thing about strong emotion.

"It will take us five minutes to pack." Richard's voice was husky. "Quickly—this way."

Bess

I NEVER KNEW, really, what happened in Rulumpur.

There was no gossip about it. And even when Dr. Broughton, the adjutant, and Lieutenant Hayes came riding in, they just shook their heads.

"You know how it is, half the Prince's entourage doesn't speak English, and we can't speak their language all that well," Dr. Broughton told me when I asked. "Your father straightened it out."

"What sort of problem was it?"

"Oh, I don't know. Something to do with a child's toy the Princess's little daughter dropped along the road. The soldier who found and returned it tried to explain what he was doing, but the Prince's people accused him of stealing it." He smiled. "Could have caused no end of trouble."

Lieutenant Hayes said, when I encountered him later on the parade ground, "Bess, you know how sensitive of their dignity these Princes are. The Colonel smoothed it over. Turned out just fine—that's all that matters."

My parents had stayed in Delhi for several days, and Simon

was with them. Arrangements were being made to mark the passing of the King, and I wasn't surprised that the Colonel Sahib would wish to pay his respects.

Still, when they did come home, they looked very tired. As did Simon.

My mother laughed, and said, "Well, you know cities. No one seems to sleep. But we were expecting there would be a Book of Condolences to sign for the King's death. Still, I'm glad to be home again. Trains are all well and good, but they are also dusty and tiring." After a kiss for me, she added, "Your father took the opportunity to order new uniforms, and Simon decided to do the same. Meanwhile, I found a lovely dress for you. I'll show you after dinner."

I didn't see Simon for several days. He was kept busy writing reports, according to my father.

"Well, he was away for some days. Best to catch up before there's more trouble on the Frontier," he said. "When the Princess decides to go back to Rulumpur, it will all be to do over again, the caravan. I'm not looking forward to it."

"She's not going up to the hill country? I thought the Prince had taken a house up there during May and June."

"I expect she'll go when she's ready." And then he asked, "Did you spend much time with her?"

"I only saw her twice. Her mother was keeping her close. But she was upset about something. I couldn't help but wonder—do you think she and the Prince were having problems? I heard her quarreling with her mother the last afternoon. And Parvati was shouting. I could have sworn she said something about Simon. But then she was going on about her son and something about England. So, I must have been wrong."

We'd just finished breakfast, and Mother had gone up. He paused at the dining room door. "How did you come across that bit of information about the ayah's brother?"

"Was it useful?"

"As a matter of fact, it was. We learned that the poor man had died in an accident when he was a child."

"Oh—I'm sorry. I told you I was waiting for Parvati to come into the gardens, but she and her mother were still quarreling, so I walked a little way toward the summerhouse. I found the woman by herself, crying. I had no idea who she was, until she told me she couldn't bear to leave the little girl, that she had been there when she was born. Then I gathered she was upset about her brother, but she was talking so fast I couldn't make all of it out. And the Princess was very angry with her. When she heard Parvati calling for me, she got up and ran away. But when I said something to Parvati about it, she told me the woman had upset the Maharani. I asked if it was because of the woman's brother, and she was surprised. She hadn't heard anything about a brother. But she made it clear she didn't want to talk about it any longer, and I could tell she was still cross with her mother. We didn't have a very pleasant afternoon, I'm afraid. When I got home, I asked Major Dudley to send a telegram for me. I hadn't learned very much, but when I mentioned the ayah, he agreed at once to send a mounted runner. I asked if she was important, and he told me that when it came to the Princes, better to be safe than sorry."

The Colonel Sahib shook his head. "Major Dudley was right. I try to stay out of anything that doesn't threaten the Regiment."

"I was rather sad I couldn't have spent a little time with her, while she was here. I never saw the baby. And I could tell that whatever was wrong, they preferred to keep it to themselves. As

I was leaving the last time, I saw the Maharani at a distance, and she didn't look any happier than Parvati." I took a deep breath. "I'd have liked to help make it right."

"I'm sorry, love. Who knows, before Parvati leaves, she may send for you."

But I knew she wouldn't. We no longer had much in common. And the little boy I'd played with when he was a baby had a tutor now, and was learning to be a Prince.

When Simon was finally free of reports and came late one afternoon to play tennis with me, I asked him what had been happening. "You were with the caravan, then went to Rulumpur. Did you think that Parvati has changed?"

He smiled. "We barely spoke. She outranks both of us now. A husband, two children, a Princely kingdom all her own? I expect she's too polite to say so. She was always well-mannered."

Changing the subject, I asked, "How was Delhi?"

"Quiet. Everyone was in mourning after the King's death. Your mother went shopping one afternoon, and your father and I ordered new uniforms."

Parvati didn't leave for the hill country. Instead she finally decided to go back to Rulumpur before the monsoon rains turned the roads into bogs. In spite of everything, I went back to the Maharani's hoping to say goodbye to her. She was polite but distracted. One of the baby's nurses had been sent for by the Rajamata, and the little girl was crying for her. I asked if this was the same ayah whose brother had died, but Parvati didn't seem to know.

My father accompanied the caravan this time, with several of the junior officers. I don't know whether he spoke to Parvati or not, but it was efficiently managed this time and he was home again as soon as the train departed.

The rainy season came with its downpours. No one held dinner parties then. It was enough to survive the heat and the danger of malaria. But when it had ended and the dry season made the roads passable again, we only saw the Maharani once more.

"Did you and the Maharani have a falling-out?" I asked my mother. "You haven't been to the Palace, and she hasn't come here to call."

"Darling, no. I expect we've both been busy." She was arranging flowers for the dinner table.

"There's been no news of Parvati either. Do you think the Prince put her away? To marry again? I wouldn't care to see her unhappy." I began to set the table as we talked.

My mother smiled. "He probably wouldn't dare. Politically it wouldn't do to make the Maharani an enemy. And Parvati is the mother of the Prince's heirs."

"I'm glad for her sake. But I've often wondered . . ."

"Wondered what?" she asked when I didn't go on.

"She married as she was expected to marry. But I had a feeling that she would have preferred to marry for love."

My mother set the flowers in the center of the table. "Really? Was there someone else she cared for? There were several other young heirs who were eligible."

"She never mentioned anyone to me. Of course, she probably couldn't tell me such a thing—I wasn't old enough to know to keep her secrets. But she said once that if she ever had a daughter, she would let her choose her own husband."

"Really?" my mother said again. "Well, the Prince will probably have something to say to that, I'm sure."

And then it was time to dress for dinner, and I was looking forward to wearing that new gown for the first time.

I THOUGHT SIMON had changed since the visit to Delhi. I couldn't quite decide how or why.

When I said something to my father about that, he laughed.

"I expect being Sergeant Major has had something to do with that. He's very young for that honor. But the ranks like him."

"Well, he's had several years to grow used to his new rank." I hesitated. "He's not reconsidering going to Sandhurst, is he? I'd be glad for him, of course, but I know all of us would miss him terribly."

"He's said nothing about that to me. Has he mentioned it to you?"

"No."

"Has he treated you any differently?"

"I don't think so. We were quarreling only yesterday about something. He treats me like his little sister. And I'm not." Before he could say anything, I added, "I'll be fourteen in a few weeks. I'd like to be friends instead."

I could have sworn my father smothered a smile—it was a rather choking cough—and I said crossly, "Is that such a difficult thing to ask?"

"Well, I expect that will happen. Will you be putting your hair up and begin riding sidesaddle and stop outshooting half the ranks?"

I had to laugh. "I expect Miss would be glad if I did." I knew there were times when my governess despaired of me. But there was so much of interest to me, and so many things I enjoyed doing out here. Sitting quietly embroidering handkerchiefs for my parents or practicing the piano or painting watercolors of different flowers was all very well, and I was good at them, but I was my father's daughter, and I loved the Regiment as much as he did.

Which is why, when something else happened late that year, I was quite surprised, although I think my mother saw it coming.

We were due to rotate back to Hampshire in late November, and saying goodbye to India was going to be difficult for me.

My father had finally brokered a truce with the worst of the raiding tribes, and he could leave with an easy mind that all would be well out here. There was talk of the Regiment going to South Africa next, and the ranks were excited about that.

Then why, when we finally reached London in early December, had my father resigned? And Simon along with him?

I asked my mother about that, and she'd answered me honestly, I thought.

"The politics of India had disappointed him, I think. He'd felt let down by that. When we went to Delhi, that time, he was angry with some of the Governor-General's staff. They'd put political interests ahead of his men when he'd asked for their help. And you know how your father has always felt, that the Regiment came first."

"He's too young to retire to Somerset and grow marrows," I'd said.

"He'll find something to keep him busy. Never fear. And Simon as well."

I'd said something to Simon about his future. But he'd shaken his head. "I've been a soldier long enough, Bess. The Regiment gave me something I'd been looking for. I'm grateful for that. But your father is right. It's time to leave."

It wasn't until much, much later, that I was told the truth.

That neither the Governor-General nor his staff had had the time to consider my father's concerns for his men. He couldn't walk away then—he still had his duty ahead of him. Not until that was finished, would he be free to go.

Even though London tried very hard to persuade both my father and Simon to stay, it would take a war to bring the Colonel Sahib back to the Army. And Simon as well. But that was still four years in the future . . .

We came home to Somerset to find that Iris and the dailies had taken all the dust covers off the furniture and the chandeliers. The bedding had been aired, the rooms dusted within an inch of their lives. And my father was happier than I'd seen him for years.

I was afraid that Simon would go home to his own family, even though he'd never talked to me about them or his childhood. But he seemed quite pleased to retire to the cottage beyond the wood at the bottom of our garden. And he was in and out of our house just as he'd always been. I'd often watched the two of them together and thought how alike they were, as if Simon were the son my father had never had. I said something about that to my mother one morning when the Colonel Sahib and Simon were trying to set up a swing for us under a tree in the back garden.

She had smiled, and said only, "Yes, that's rather nice, isn't it?" Then she turned to me and said, "You don't mind?"

"I'm happy for both of them. Melinda told me when she came to visit last week that she thought she had met Simon once in Hampshire. Before he was sent out to India. I asked Simon about that, and he told me he'd escorted her to meet one of the officers there."

"I'm not surprised. She's kept up with the Regiment, even though she's a widow. It was her home for so many years."

I could appreciate that—I'd found it hard at first to fit into the quiet life of a young lady, having been accustomed to the freedom I'd enjoyed in India, but I soon made friends among the families within riding distance. Simon teased me about my beaux, the brothers and cousins of those friends. I didn't know then how many of them I'd lose to war in only a few years' time.

The fighting the Regiment had seen on the North-West Frontier would put them into the forefront of that war, and I couldn't sit idly by while those men were being wounded and killed. And that was why, in the early days of September 1914, I had gone to London, and with my parents' blessing, applied to become a nurse. My father had always done his duty, and now it was my turn as well.

Look for the next entry in the
Bess Crawford mystery series

AN IRISH HOSTAGE

Coming Summer 2021

and

read on for a sneak peek at Charles Todd's next
Inspector Ian Rutledge mystery

A FATAL LIE

Coming February 2021

1

The River Dee, Llangollen Valley
Early Spring 1921

ON HIS SIXTH birthday, Roddy MacNabb was given a fishing pole by his pa, with promises to teach him how to use it. That was late July 1914, before the Bloody Hun started the war, and his pa had left the village with four of his friends and enlisted. He'd promised to be back before the end of the year, but the war had dragged on, and in 1915, his father had been killed at Bloody Passiondell, wherever that was.

The pole, long since put away, was in his granny's attics, and Roddy had only just found it last week, when he'd gone up there to fetch a box for her. He'd brought it down with him, but his mum had told him to take the Bloody Pole out to the shed and leave it there.

"There's to be no fishing," she'd told him. "Not while you're in school."

He'd watched his granny's mouth tighten at his mother's words.

She didn't hold with cursing, but Mum had come from Liverpool, and he'd heard his Aunt May say that she'd been no better than she ought to be. Still, his father had somehow fallen in love with her and brought her home, and she'd stayed.

He didn't remember his real mum, she'd died when he was born. But his pa had told him this was his mum now, and he was to call her that. And so he had, because his pa was the best in the village, and he would have done anything to make him happy.

On Saturday, with no school and the schoolmaster ill with a chest, Roddy slipped away while his mum was having her usual late breakfast, took the fishing pole from the shed, and went off to the river.

The Dee here was within walking distance of the farm, and Roddy found himself thinking about his pa and fishing. He'd gone with his father a few times and still had a vague memory of what to do with the pole, once the hook was affixed to the line and a worm was put on it. He'd surreptitiously dug some worms out of the kitchen garden last night and put them into a tin. Most had crawled out, but there were still three left.

Whistling now, he could glimpse the river shining in the noon sun beyond the line of trees, and he told himself his father would be happy if he could see how tall his son had grown, and only twelve. And off to fish at last.

The sun was warm, but under the trees—their bare branches crossing over his head like the bones of wood holding up the church roof—the air was cooler. Or perhaps it was the water—he could hear it and smell it now. He came out onto the bank, stiff with the dried grasses of winter, and stood looking down at the drifting current. Too steep here to fish, he thought, and moved downstream a little, beyond the Telford Aqueduct soaring high above the valley.

Everyone knew the Aqueduct, but unlike the Roman ones he'd read about in school, which were intended to carry drinking water, it bridged the wide gap between two cliffs, and made it possible for the narrowboats traveling along the canal up there to float right across from one side to the other. He'd heard the horses that pulled the narrowboats, the hollow sound their hooves made as they stepped out onto the path that ran beside the trough of water. It echoed, on a quiet day. He'd been afraid the first time he'd heard it, but his pa had told him about the horses, and once had even taken him up there to see the long boats and the ducks too. He barely remembered it now, that trip, but his father had bought him an ice and told him not to tell Mum.

Ahead was a lower spot on the bank, and Roddy moved quickly toward it, eager to try out the pole and catch his fish. He didn't notice what was in the water, not at first. He wasn't interested in the river, only the pole.

After two attempts he got the line on the pole, tied the hook to the end, then pushed the wriggling worm onto the hook. On his first try at casting, he caught the bush behind him, untangled the line finally, and tried again. This time he managed better, and the hook actually sailed out over the water and sank into the sunny depths.

Smiling, he wiggled the pole a little, felt it catch, and burst out laughing. He'd caught a fish, first thing! What would his pa think of that?

But when he tried to pull the line in, it wouldn't come, and as he pulled harder, he saw something move in the water, just below the surface. From where he stood, it appeared to be a rock or even a tangle of roots.

Whatever it was, it bobbed a little as he went on pulling, harder now, desperate to save his only hook, then it suddenly came free from whatever was holding it down.

And as it did, a face rose slowly out of the water. A face unlike any other he'd ever seen, white and torn and no longer human. Like something the water had taken and hadn't ever wanted to give back. The lump of whatever was attached to it rolled a little again, making the head move as well, and for an instant Roddy thought it was coming directly out of the water at him. He screamed as he dropped the pole and ran.

But no one on the narrowboat crossing high above his head heard him.

2

CHIEF SUPERINTENDENT MARKHAM was in a fine mood. He had been congratulated twice on the successful conclusion of a rather nasty murder inquiry in Norfolk—once by the Home Office, and again in an article in the *Times*.

Inspector Carlton had brought in the killer, covering himself with glory as well as the Yard, and he was currently basking in the Chief Superintendent's smile.

Inspector Rutledge, on the other hand, was still in his office, buried in paperwork. His last inquiry had stirred up a mare's nest, and Markham was apparently still smarting from that, because he'd seen to it for several weeks that Rutledge wasn't given a new assignment.

Rutledge had not complained—much to Markham's annoyance, according to Sergeant Gibson.

When the Chief Constable in a northern Welsh county asked the Yard to take charge of an inquiry into the death of a man found in the River Dee, Markham summoned Rutledge to his office, brusquely told him what was required of him, and said,

"Sergeant Gibson will see that someone takes over the reports you were reviewing." He passed the file across the desk, nodded, and began to read another report already open on the green blotter. The air was chill with Markham's dislike.

Rutledge extricated himself from the office as smoothly as he could, collected what he needed from his own room, and informed Sergeant Gibson of the status of the reports on his desk.

Gibson grimaced. "Does this mean you're back in his lordship's good graces?"

"I doubt it. Northern Wales is rather like being sent to Coventry—out of sight and out of mind."

Gibson nodded. "There's that."

It was a Monday morning, overcast, cold. As he walked out of the Yard to his motorcar, Rutledge could smell the Thames, fetid with the receding tide. At his flat, he packed a valise, left a note for the daily, and then headed west through dreary outskirts and a succession of small towns before he reached open countryside.

By that time he was no longer able to ignore the voice coming from the rear seat.

It wasn't there, that voice. He knew it as clearly as he could see the ruts in the road unwinding ahead of the motorcar's bonnet. Corporal Hamish MacLeod was buried in the black mud of Flanders, and Rutledge had once stood by that grave and contemplated his own mortality.

It was the manner of Hamish's death that haunted him, and the guilt of that had turned into denial. By the end of the war he had brought Hamish home to England in the only way possible, *knowing* he was dead, but unable to free himself of the voice that had stayed with him in the trenches from the Battle of the Somme to the Armistice. It had followed him relentlessly, sometimes bitter, sometimes angry, and sometimes, for a mercy, even bearable. But always there. And with it, the memories of the war.

What he, Rutledge, feared above all was one day seeing the owner of the voice—and knowing beyond doubt that he had finally run mad. The only answer to that was the service revolver locked in the chest under his bed at the flat.

For it was he who had delivered the coup de grace that silenced Hamish forever. Military necessity. But even as Hamish had broken during the Somme, he himself had been on the ragged edge of shell shock. England had needed every man that July. No one walked back to the forward aid station and asked for relief from the horror. They withstood it as best they could, week after unbearable week, and hoped for death when the agony was too much.

Hamish was saying, "Ye ken, the Yard doubts ye. Else, they'd no' send ye to Wales for a drowning."

Rutledge didn't answer.

"Aye, ye can try to ignore the signs. But ye've seen them for yersel'."

Hamish was trying to goad him into a quarrel, but it was only a reflection of his own troubled mind.

Setting his teeth, he concentrated on the road ahead. There was nothing Hamish could say that he hadn't heard before, or thought, or dreamed of at night. Tried to ignore—but could never put completely out of his mind. It was there, had been since the trenches. A constant reminder of the war and what he'd done on that bloody nightmare of the Somme. Seemingly as real as if the living Hamish MacLeod traveled with him.

Rutledge could feel that presence growing stronger as he made his way into the Cotswolds. Waiting for him as it always did at the end of a long day. He had wanted to drive another twenty or so miles, but as he found himself in a village of butter-yellow stone reflecting the last of the evening light, he knew that it wasn't possible. There was a small, charming inn near the village center—as good a place as any to face the night. He ate his dinner in a dining room that was only half full. The food was good, the whisky with his tea even better, and he found himself relaxing for the first time in a very long while. Hoping it would last and he would sleep after all.

A woman across the room laughed. His back was to her, he couldn't see her face, but the laugh was rather like Kate's when she was truly amused. His whisky glass halfway to his lips, he paused, caught off guard.

But Kate was in London . . .

Setting his glass down, unfinished, he went up to the small room where Hamish was waiting in the shadows for him.

It was a long night. He'd been having nightmares more frequently of late, Hamish drawing him back into the war, filling him with guilt and despair and a longing for peace that always left him drained in the first light of dawn. As if in the blackness surrounding him the past came back more easily, slipping through the darkness in the room and in him until he couldn't hold it back any longer.

His last thought as the nightmare took its firm grip on his mind was, *How could I ever do this to Kate? How could I ever let her see this part of me?*

RUTLEDGE ARRIVED AT his destination, Cwmafon, on a Wednesday afternoon of soaking rain and lowering clouds that turned everything gray and dismal. Much like his own mood. In spite of a good sense of direction, as he'd driven deeper into northern Wales, he'd struggled with place-names he couldn't pronounce and others that weren't even on the English map he'd brought with him.

He finally found the country lane that followed the River Dee into the village he was after, saw the tiny police station next to a general store, and splashed through the puddles to the door.

The Constable behind the desk looked up as the door opened and a wet stranger stepped in.

"Good afternoon, sir. Constable Holcomb. How may I be of service?" He rose to meet the newcomer.

"Inspector Rutledge, Scotland Yard," he replied as he took off his hat and glanced down ruefully at the circle of rainwater expanding on the mat under his feet.

Holcomb smiled. "You made good time, sir. Never mind the rain. It's gone on for three days, but we are hoping for a bit of sun by tomorrow." There was a soft Welsh lilt to his voice, but he was a fair man, broad-shouldered and stocky in build.

"That's good news."

Gesturing to the chair across from him, Holcomb sat down again. "Sorry to say, there's no good news about the body the boy found. We haven't identified him yet. Dr. Evans says he'd been in the river a few days, which hasn't helped. And from the look of him, we think he must have fallen from the Aqueduct. There was a lot of damage internally, consistent with such a fall. It's a long way."

He'd seen the Aqueduct. A towering array of arches with the top only a faint outline in the low clouds. "That puts his death around Thursday of last week."

"Yes, sir. I've made inquiries," the Constable went on. "But no one is missing from up there. No narrowboat owner or passenger, no visitor to the site. No stranger wandering about. You can walk across the Aqueduct, along the horse path. Easy to lose one's balance, looking down. If he fell at night, there might not have been anyone to see him start out—or go over."

"And no one missing down here?"

"Nor here," Holcomb agreed.

"Then we've not got much to be going on with."

The Constable sighed. "Sadly so, I'm afraid." Frowning, he added, "There was another case very like this one, three years ago. A body found on Mount Snowdon, spotted in a hollow by a sharp-eyed young woman on the cog railway to the summit. The little train hadn't run for several days—weather coming down—or likely he'd have been found earlier. A hiker, judging from his clothing, presumably caught in the storm. Took two months to prove it was a suicide. The Chief Constable has a long memory, sir. He'd like to see this inquiry concluded sooner rather than later."

Rutledge smiled grimly, thinking that the Chief Constable and Chief Superintendent Markham had much in common. He asked, "Any reason to believe our body was a suicide?"

"Not yet, sir. For one thing, he wasn't dressed for hiking. Nor did he appear to be down on his luck, as far as we can tell. But then you never know, do you, sir?" Holcomb rose. "A cuppa tea wouldn't go amiss just now, sir, given the day?"

"Thank you, Constable." Although the room was warm enough as it was, almost too warm.

Holcomb moved the kettle on a shelf above the small stove to its top, then poured in water from a jug sitting on the floor. As he busied himself with the cups and saucers, he added, "Roddy

MacNabb is a good lad. The one who found the man in the river. Gave him a nasty shock, that did. He'd taken out a fishing pole, hoping to give it a try, and found a corpse instead. His gran sent for Dr. Evans, who had to give the lad something to calm him down a bit before they'd even got round to what he'd seen. Roddy was convinced the body was coming up out of the water after him. Which of course it never did. Dr. Evans discovered later that the hook from the pole had caught in the man's clothes, and as the lad pulled at what he thought was a fish, the body moved."

"How is the boy now?"

"Well enough. His gran wouldn't let him go to school. The other lads would have swarmed him, asking questions, which would bring it all back again." The kettle whistled and he set about making the tea. Bringing Rutledge a cup and then taking his own back to the desk, he sat down again. "There is one other thing. Roddy's stepmother. She's not from around here. MacNabb met her in Liverpool or some such before the war, brought her home, and married her. Against all advice. Still, he was a good man. Killed in the war. I wasn't all that surprised when Mrs. MacNabb wondered if the dead man might have something to do with her daughter-in-law."

Surprised, Rutledge said, "And does he, do you think?"

Holcomb frowned. "Begging your pardon, sir, but I don't believe the dead man is her sort. There have been a few rumors over the years about Rosie MacNabb, none proved. She has a taste for trouble, you might say. Usually the sort that comes in trousers. But she's been careful never to push her mother-in-law far enough to send her packing. The feeling is that there was nothing much in Liverpool to draw her back. She'd as soon stay."

"Then why is this man not her sort?"

"He was short, sir. Just a bit over five feet." He considered the man across from him. "Rosie prefers them tall."

BY THE TIME they had finished their tea, the rain had stopped, but the clouds overhead were still heavy with moisture. Holcomb took Rutledge to the doctor's surgery, several houses down the road from the police station. Water stood everywhere, mirroring the gloomy sky. The house itself was not very large, but it was connected to a smaller cottage next door by an enclosed passage. The Constable led the way up the walk to the cottage. Knocking at the door, he waited. A woman came to answer the summons.

She was matronly, with a pretty face, dark hair, and a competent air about her.

"Afternoon, Mrs. Evans," Holcomb was saying. "I've brought the Inspector from London to speak to the doctor."

"Of course." She smiled at Rutledge, then led them through a waiting room to the office beyond. Opening the door after a brief tap, she thrust her head in and said, "It's the Constable, my dear, with the man up from London."

"Send them in." The voice was gruff.

She opened the door wider, and the two men went inside. Dr. Evans was standing beside the mantelpiece, knocking the dottle from his pipe into the fire. He straightened, stuck the empty pipe into his pocket, and nodded to them.

He was older than his wife, graying, fifty perhaps, with spectacles that didn't hide the sharpness of eyes so dark they seemed to be black.

"Inspector Rutledge, Dr. Evans," Rutledge said, holding out his hand, and Evans shook it before settling them in front of his desk. Mrs. Evans had shut the door and gone away.

"Not much to tell you," he said, in the same gruff manner. "Dead, clearly fell from a high place. Given where he was found, that would most certainly be the Aqueduct. No water in his lungs to speak of, he didn't drown. But my guess is that he was in the Dee for two or three days."

"Was he alive when he fell? Or had he been killed and then dropped over the edge of the Aqueduct?"

"That's harder to judge. The river didn't do him any favors. Between that and his fall, any bruising or other signs of a struggle would be masked by the massive injuries he sustained almost immediately afterward. If he was alive, I suspect he saw his death coming. It's a long drop. Not a very pleasant thought." He shook his head. "Nasty business."

"Was there enough left of his face for a description?"

"I can only tell you that he had light brown hair, brown eyes, was barely five feet tall, and that three ribs had previously been cracked and healed with time. Age in his early thirties, I should think. You can see him, if you like. I doubt it will do you any good."

"Yes, I'd like to have a look. You are certain about where he fell from?"

"Given finding him in the water with those injuries, there was no other conclusion to draw. The only other possibility is having fallen from an aircraft. And Holcomb here can tell you there were none of those flying about in the week before he was discovered."

Rutledge glanced toward the Constable, saw the shake of his head, and turned back to Evans. "Anything about his clothing that might be helpful in finding out who he was?"

"Dark suit, not of the best quality but presentable enough. English made, I expect. There's a label in the shirt, but not, I think, from a known tailor. Holcomb here asked around, but no one seems to recognize the maker. The body was wearing no watch or ring, no watch chain. Of course, he might have had those, and they are either at the bottom of the Dee or in the pocket of whoever killed him—if, of course, this was murder. Not even a purse or loose coins in his pockets. One handkerchief, coarse linen, no initials. His boots were of good leather, reasonable wear and tear on the sole, and there was a hole in the right stocking, at the toe."

It was an oddly human finding.

"No overcoat, this time of year? Or hat?"

"No. He might well have left them somewhere. Or perhaps his killer took them."

Holcomb interjected, "We've searched for any belongings. All along the river where he might have come down. And a swath on either side of the banks. I've had local men out there looking. They know the Dee, they would have found a hat or coat. Or anything else."

"I must be sure. You're confident they were thorough?" Rutledge asked.

"We even went farther downstream in case some belongings drifted on, after the body lodged in the shallows."

Rutledge turned back to the doctor. "Murder? Or accident?"

"Impossible to say, medically. If he fell by accident, he'd have had some form of identification with him, surely. Still, if he didn't want to be identified, a suicide, he took care to see that he wasn't. If it was murder, his killer stripped him of anything useful to us. And that's what I reported to the Chief Constable. This death was probably not an accident." Dr. Evans rose. "Again I warn you, it isn't pleasant, what you're about to see. And he's been dead a week." He went to a cabinet, took out a small bottle of disinfectant, soaked three squares of gauze in it, and held out two of them. "You will be glad of this."

The back room, where the body was lying on a table, reeked of decayed flesh. Rutledge's mouth tightened as he recognized it and was for a moment back in the trenches, where the smell of rotting bodies had been omnipresent to the point of being commonplace. Unavoidable, and therefore best ignored. He held up the small square of gauze, as Holcomb and the doctor were doing. It wasn't a great deal of help.

The body was as Evans had said, badly damaged and in the river too long. It wouldn't have bloated, given the fall, sinking to the bottom of the river and moving with the current until it lodged in roots or against rocks.

Evans was right, also, that there was too little left of the face, reminding Rutledge of a leper he'd seen in France. He found himself thinking that the dead man's family wouldn't have recognized what was left. But the heavy bone at the nose, the squared line of the skeletal chin were indications of a strong face. On the other hand, brown hair and eyes were common enough in Wales and on the Welsh borders.

The man's clothing had been folded neatly on a smaller table against the wall, but it too smelled, as Rutledge touched the fabric of the man's suit and looked at the black boots. The handmade label stitched into the neckband of the shirt was faded, not new, but he could read the ornate script: *Banner.* Just beneath it was what appeared to be the tailor's mark, a needle with a loop of thread through the eye. He took out his notebook and made a rough sketch of the design.

The dead man had been dressed, he thought, to conduct business somewhere, not to take up work. Not a laborer, then. Turning away, he said, "Anything else that we can use?"

Evans gestured to the left arm. "There is one thing, but I doubt it will be helpful. On the forearm, just there. I can't make out what it might be."

Rutledge leaned closer for a better look. The skin was broken, bits missing. But there *was* something. Holcomb came up to peer at it over his shoulder.

"It's not the same color as the skin around it. A tattoo, do you think?" Rutledge looked up at the doctor. "In the war, were you?"

Evans shook his head.

"It was a popular thing among the ranks. A sweetheart's name, one's regiment, a battle." Straightening up, Rutledge added, "I can't be sure, of course. But I think that's what we're seeing here. Do you have a magnifying glass?"

Evans nodded, opening a drawer against the wall. "Will this do?"

It was small, but Rutledge took it and held it over the dark patch. It magnified the rotting skin as much as it did the faded pattern. He handed the glass to Holcomb as he went on. "My guess is that our unknown body *was* in the war. And given how short he is, I'd say that could very well be the insignia of the Bantam Battalions."

Pressing the square of gauze hard against his nose, Holcomb peered at the discoloration. "I can't say I can make out a bantam rooster. Looks more like a"—he searched for the right comparison—"like a tree, don't you think? An oak, perhaps?"

Oaks were a popular tattoo, given their association with the Stuart King Charles II hiding in an oak tree during his escape from England and the clutches of Cromwell. Any number of pubs and inns had been named for that tree. There was even, Rutledge remembered, a Revenge-class battleship brought into service in November 1914 named *Royal Oak*.

Had the dead man served on her? It might prove to be the link between the body and the narrowboats. Had he once worked on them, before the war?

Ignoring the smell, Rutledge looked more closely at the faint pattern. Oak—or rooster?

The tree was generally shown in full leaf, and with a massive spread of roots below, the same width and depth as the tree was wide and tall.

The Bantam tattoo, as he remembered it, showed the rooster above with larger entwined *B*s below it.

But so much of the skin was missing, it was hard to determine any size here. He looked away, then returned to his inspection. There—at the bottom left. Was that the straight line of a *B*? There were no straight lines in roots . . .

Rutledge looked away once more, staring at the wall for an instant, then turned back to the arm before him. Leaves went up. A rooster's tail went down. He thought he could just pick out the faint blue line of half a feather.

The smell was getting to him, the trenches, the dead—

He moved back, trying to evade the odor of decaying death, but it seemed to be everywhere, distinctive, cloying, strong.

Taking a grip on the sudden flood of memories, he forced himself to think clearly.

There was nothing in what little was left of the design to indicate a tree. But there were a straight line and then a downward line with three short lines perpendicular to it. A possible *B*—a possible feather.

"I think not," Rutledge said, answering Holcomb. "But given

the number of shorter men finally allowed to enlist in the Army by Kitchener, it doesn't narrow our search all that much. And short men were allowed to join the Navy, in due course."

"Well," said Holcomb, stepping back and handing the glass to Evans, "I'm fair flummoxed. It could be a tattoo right enough. I'll give you that. But I'm damned if I know what it might be showing."

Dr. Evans said, "The only thing in the Inspector's favor is the fact that the top appears to be larger on the right than on the left. A rooster has a small head to the left, large body in the center, and larger tail to the right. Still, that could be a problem with the torn skin and not the design."

"There's little else to be going forward with. I'll look into the Bantams to see if the body can be identified through the regiments."

Holcomb shot him a look of relief as Rutledge started for the door. Evans followed, with Holcomb at his heels, coughing sharply.

The air in the passage seemed fresh and sweet by comparison as the doctor shut the door firmly behind them. Back in the office, Evans didn't sit down.

"I've given you all I can. I don't recognize this man, and nor does Holcomb, and we know most of the men in the village and on the surrounding farms. Besides that, so far we have no missing person query. I don't think our body is actually ours. You'd be better off inquiring among the narrowboats that cross on the Aqueduct."

Beyond the door to the waiting room, Rutledge could hear voices, and so could the doctor. Patients waiting.

Hamish spoke suddenly, jarring Rutledge.

"He's no' a man wi' imagination, yon doctor."

Holcomb glanced at Rutledge, who said briskly, covering his reaction, "Thank you, Dr. Evans. If I have more questions, I'll be in touch."

"Can't think what they might be, but you'll be welcome to come again."

And then they were passing through the curious stares in the crowded waiting room and out onto the street.

Holcomb looked back at the closed door of the surgery, then said, "Well, he's right, I expect. It's our body because the poor sod landed here. But not our inquiry, do you think? Sir?"

A man no one wanted. The thought passed through Rutledge's mind. Inconveniently dead on their patch.

Or was he?

Time would tell.

"At the moment, he's still ours." They started in the direction of the station. "Who should I speak to at the Aqueduct?"

"I've not spent much time up there. Once after a thief who'd strayed our way. He'd been robbing the boats over that winter. Went with my brother another time when he was looking for work." He shrugged. "We don't have that much in common with the narrowboat folks."

"Where is your brother now? Did he find work there?"

"No, no experience handling the craft. But it was worth a try, he kept telling me he wasn't cut out for farming. Until of course he met a lass who was a farmer's daughter." He cleared his throat. "Lost him in the war, died of gangrene during the Somme Offensive."

It had been hot that July, the dying and the dead everywhere, and no time to save half of them. It would have been easy to die as gangrene set in, taking the leg and then the man.

Shutting out the past with an effort, Rutledge nodded. "I'm sorry."

Holcomb shrugged. "Nice memorial brass in the chapel so he'll be remembered. But I'd rather have had him home, leg or no leg."

They finished the short walk in silence.

"You'll want to speak to the lad who found the body," Holcomb said when they reached the police station.

"Yes." He glanced at his watch. "This should be as good a time as any."

"He can't add much to what the doctor told you, but he's a good lad, and still shaken by what happened."

Rutledge crossed to the motorcar. "You'll show me the way?"

"Happy to, sir." He turned the crank for Rutledge and then got in beside him.

"Straight through the village, and the first left. After that, it's not far."

The farmhouse sat back in a windbreak of mature trees that must have been planted at the time it was built. Gray stone, a slate roof, and an urn of early pansies by the door. It could have been any one of the farms Rutledge had passed, driving into Wales.

A woman came to the door as they stepped out of the motorcar. She was tall, with graying hair that still had a hint of dark red in it, and an attractive face that was lined with worry at the moment.

Holcomb said in a low voice, "Her husband's great-grandfather came from Scotland to work on the Aqueduct. MacNabb. Met a Welsh lass and married her. When the work was done on the Aqueduct, he stayed."

Rutledge was taking off his hat. "Mrs. MacNabb? My name is Rutledge. I've been sent by Scotland Yard to look into the death of the man your grandson found by the river."

She nodded to Holcomb, then said quietly to Rutledge, "We were expecting you to call. My grandson has nightmares now. I hope you'll be gentle with him." And she opened the door wider, to allow them to step in.

The parlor was lit by windows on two sides, today letting in only the gray light, but Rutledge could picture it on a sunny day, the yellow-and-lavender wallpaper reflecting it in every corner.

Over the mantel in pride of place was a painting of a man in Highland kit, standing by a loch where trees climbed the surrounding hills.

She saw Rutledge's glance and smiled slightly. "My husband's great-grandfather's father, and mine. I'm a cousin as well as a wife. It was sent to him after his father's death. I sometimes think its purpose was to make my great-grandfather homesick. But they hadn't seen eye to eye in life, and there was nothing for Robbie back there." Abruptly changing the subject, she said, "May I offer you tea?"

"Thank you, no," Rutledge said, smiling and taking one of the overstuffed chairs she indicated. "I think it best if we keep our visit short."

She nodded. "I won't be a moment." And then she was back with the gangling boy of eleven or twelve who had gone fishing and found a dead man.

His face was rather pale, and a sprinkle of freckles stood out across his nose. He said politely in a low voice, "How do you do?"

Holcomb leaned forward, but Rutledge was there before he could speak. "Hallo. Roddy, is it? My name is Rutledge, I've come from London to find out what I can about the man you discovered. It would help me search for answers if you could tell me a little about what happened to you."

It wasn't what the boy had expected. He said, "I can't tell you much. I hardly looked at him."

"I've seen him," Rutledge said, nodding. "It was very unpleasant. But I was wondering. Was he floating when you got to the riverbank? Or caught in the shallows somehow?"

"I don't know," Roddy replied. "I didn't see him at first. Not until my hook caught in his coat, and—and I pulled. I didn't know it—I had no idea what it was. Until he rolled over."

"It must have been a dreadful shock," Rutledge agreed. "That particular place in the river. Downstream from the Aqueduct, do you think?"

"About half a mile," the boy said, nodding. "It wasn't overhead. But I could hear sounds from up there."

"Anything or anyone in the vicinity of where you were fishing, along the river just there?"

"I don't think so." He glanced uneasily at his grandmother. "I wasn't—I shouldn't have been out there, fishing. But I found the pole, you see, and I wanted to try it. I thought it best to stay out of sight."

There had been a search of both banks, upstream and downstream, but nothing had been found, and now there was no indication that others had come searching for the dead body before Roddy's discovery.

Rutledge nodded. "I'd have done the same. Good fishing in the Dee, do you think?"

"I don't know. I hadn't tried before."

"Why did you choose that particular spot?"

"It was flatter just there, I could get to the water more easily."

"And no one had been there before you? No footprints or other signs of anyone about?"

"No. I wasn't really looking—but I'd have—I'd have moved on

if I'd seen other people." He lifted a shoulder, not looking at his grandmother. "I should have been helping. It was a Saturday."

Somewhere in the house a door slammed, making the boy jump and glance anxiously at his grandmother. Before she could say anything, they heard brisk footsteps, and the door to the parlor swung open. A younger woman stepped in. Mrs. MacNabb introduced her daughter-in-law without any inflection in her voice or change in her expression, but her gray eyes were as hard as flint.

Even dressed as a farmer's widow, it was clear what sort of woman Roddy's stepmother had been. It was there in her face and the way she moved forward, her gaze on Rutledge, prepared to be the center of attention.

Roddy had moved back toward his grandmother, eyes down, looking at no one and nothing.

But before she could ask to be introduced, Rutledge rose, smiled pleasantly, and said, "Mrs. MacNabb, I believe? We were just leaving. A few questions for Roddy, in the course of my inquiries. He's a good lad. You must be quite proud of him."

Holcomb was on his feet as well, following Rutledge toward the door.

Rutledge let him pass, looked at the elder Mrs. MacNabb, and said, "Thank you. We won't trouble you again." And to Roddy, he added, "You were a brave lad."

The boy mumbled something. The grandmother followed them to the door, and shut it after them.

Rutledge strode to the motorcar. Holcomb was already turning the crank.

"I wasn't going to give her a chance to interfere," he said grimly. "If I'd found a body out here, along the river or the road, I'd not have been surprised to see it was her. I don't know how the grand-mother puts up with her. Did you learn anything from the boy?"

"Only that no one was still searching the river for the body. We can't be sure of that, of course, they could have come and gone long before Roddy went fishing."

"Falling from that height, there wouldn't be any question the man was dead."

"I don't think a murderer would have cared either way," Rut-ledge replied. "But if no one else came looking for him, it could mean he had no friends up there wondering where he'd got to. Therefore he was very likely a stranger."

But before driving back into town, Rutledge asked Holcomb to show him where the body had been drifting when Roddy MacNabb's hook brought it to light.

The sun was just struggling to break through when they reached the spot.

The ground was trampled and muddy still where the men had worked to bring the corpse in and others had come to stare. The little clearing was no longer a tempting place to stop and try for a fish. Holcomb looked around it and shook his head. "It was bad luck the dead man got caught on something here. For a killer, that is. If it'd stayed midstream, now, it might have floated well away."

"That was very likely what a killer hoped for." As Rutledge turned to go, he looked up at the graceful dark red brick aque-duct, towering far above his head, the very top section gray cast iron. He realized that the top of the structure must be where the waterway and the horse path were carried across. Eighteen slender pillars rose from the valley floor in arches that ran from right to left, bridging the gap from side to side. A span of near 1,000 feet, if he was any judge, and a good 120 feet high. Yet the waterway itself was invisible from here. In fact, at first glance one could almost believe the Romans had built it.

"Elegant piece of work, isn't it?"

"That it is." Holcomb shaded his eyes as a shout echoed from above, and another voice answered it.

"What if our man's killer waited to make his move until he was certain his victim would go into the river? Where the body had a good chance of being carried away downstream, possibly never found?" Rutledge asked thoughtfully. "If he did, it speaks of premeditation, not an argument that got out of hand. It's a place to start."

"A different world up there," the Constable agreed darkly. "Not one I know."

About the Author

CHARLES TODD is the author of the Bess Crawford mysteries, the Inspector Ian Rutledge mysteries, and two stand-alone novels. A mother-and-son writing team, they live on the East Coast.

Discover great authors, exclusive offers, and more at hc.com.